genevieve

THE GOLDEN CAT

A lifelong cat lover, Gabriel King has shared a home with every variety of feline from stray mog to pedigree. Born in Cornwall and raised in Warwickshire, the author now lives in West London with a Norwegian Forest Cat and a Burmilla.

Gabriel King's previous novel, *The Wild Road* is also available in Arrow.

D0591800

'Reading *The Wild Road* was like slipping into another culture, almost as if it had been very well translated from a feline language'
Robin Hobb

'Amongst the books which have given me great pleasure this year was Gabriel King's *The Wild Road* . . . An enthralling epic'
Peter Burton, *Gay Times*

'Don't pass this terrific book by'
Newcastle Sun

'Some of the best descriptions in modern literature . . . quite spectacular'
British Fantasy Society

'A fascinating tale'
Cat World

'Tag and his companions inhabit a landscape vividly imagined in feline terms'
The Good Book Guide

THE
GOLDEN
CAT

Gabriel King

ARROW

For all the cats that have died in the name of science. May they rest in peace.

Contents

Legend tells of a Golden Cat, a creature of great and mystical power, sought by humans through the age. One came perilously close. His name was the Alchemist.

This man pursued the Golden Cat for three hundred years, prolonging his mortal span with magic distilled from the cats he bred and discarded in his quest, until finally he managed to procure the Queen of Cats, the beautiful Pertelot Fitzwilliam, from whom the precious kitten was destined to be born.

And thus began a terrible time for catkind: for the Alchemist was determined on his course, and with his magic and his army of alchemical cats he pursued the Queen and her consort, Ragnar Gustaffson; through the wild roads and across the land. Had it not been for the courage and resourcefulness of the friends they encountered in their flight – a silver cat known simply as Tag, a brave fox and a strutting magpie; the travelling cat, Sealink, and her heroic mate, Mousebreath; and especially for the sacrifice of the Alchemist's own cat, the wise old Majicou, the fate of all felidae *would even now hang in the balance.*

But on the headland above sacred Tintagel, where the first royal cats forged the first wild roads, a momentous battle took place. At the height of that battle, the Queen's kittens were born: but even as the Alchemist strove to take them, so the Majicou struck. Together they fell; down from the cliffs, into the depths of the ocean; then up they soared into the radiant dome of the sky. Then, in a last despairing gesture, bound together like Kilkenny cats by the hatred of hundreds of years, they plunged back down to Tintagel Head, where, in an eruption of dirt and vegetation, and a hot mist of vaporised rock, they drove themselves into the earth; and the earth sealed itself over them for ever; or so it seemed . . .

From The Ninth Life of Cats

Prologue

A large gate tower once controlled access to the city from the east. Its excavated remains, reduced by time to seven or eight courses of pale grey stone, lie on the north bank not far up-river from the Fantastic Bridge. They are railed off so that human beings cannot fall in and hurt themselves. People are always to be seen here, whatever the weather. They walk about with that aimless human vigour, narrowing their eyes at things and talking their dull talk. They stare down into the asymmetric mass of the old tower. They boast about its walls – so sturdy and thick, packed with chalk ballast – as if they had built them only the other day. They draw one another's attention to the broken arrow slits, the rusty bolts, the chisel marks on the ancient stone, the doorstep clearly visible after all these years, polished by the passage of ten thousand feet.

The keep itself has a mossy, pebbled floor. Weeds infest its inner ledges, where the walls are streaked with moisture. Coins glint here and there: people have thrown them in for what they call in their dull human way 'luck'.

The children gaze down and, a little mystified by the safety rails, ask their parents: 'Are there tigers in here?'

'No dear, that's at the zoo,' the parents say. 'The tigers are only at the zoo.'

But what do they know?

One unseasonable day at the end of spring, a cat flickered briefly into existence in the ruins. He was large and muscular and had the look of an animal who lived outdoors. His coat was pale metallic grey, tipped with black and shading

From the northern bank, behind the moored barges, the sweet smell of hawthorn rolled towards him. Something moved on one of the moored barges: but it was only an ancient tabby barge-cat with arthritic legs, fidgeting among the polished brass fitments under a line of damp washing.

Was it here?

No.

He visited a burned-down warehouse in the docklands south of the river – appearing briefly at the base of a wall, nothing but a shadow, nothing but the filmy grey image of a cat caught turning away, dissolving back into the scaly old brickwork even as he arrived.

It wasn't there, either.

Finally he set himself to face the east, and an abandoned pet shop in a place called Cutting Lane.

He stood uncertainly in the gloom, as he always did when he came here. A few feeble rays of light fell across the black-ened wooden floors. There were faint smells of dust and mice, even fainter ones of straw and animal feed: and – there! – beneath it all, the smell of a human with a broom, long ago. If he listened, he could hear the broom scrape, scrape, scrape at the rats' nests of straw in the corners. He could smell a white sixteen-week kitten in a pen. The kitten was himself. Here he had taunted the rabbits and guinea pigs, eyed speculatively the captive finches. How they had chattered and sworn at him! He was always unsure what to feel about it all. Here his fortune had changed. Here the one-eyed black cat called Majicou had found him a home and changed his life for ever. He still shivered to think of it.

'Majicou?' he whispered.

But he knew that the Majicou was long gone.

He sat down. He looked from corner to empty corner. He watched the motes dance in the rays of light. He thought hard. The colour of his eyes changed slowly from jade to the lambent green of electricity.

'Something is wrong with the wild roads,' he told himself. 'But I don't know what it is.'

ner. He went up until he stood at the top of the house, at the entrance to the room below the copper dome. The door had jammed open two or three inches the last time it was used, but Tag knew he would not go in. He had tried and failed too many times before. In there, the copper dome brooded a gathering night: in there, silence itself would bring an echo. Cold draughts flowed out even on a warm day, and the air was heavy with something that made his eyes water.

In there, the Alchemist had worked for centuries to make the Golden Cat.

Tag shivered.

He remembered Majicou again, and the events that had led, not so long before, to Majicou's death on Tintagel Head. Nothing could be concluded from those events. While something had ended there, Tag knew, nothing had been solved. This new mystery was a part of it. If there was an answer, much of it lay before him, for the faint, cold stink of the Alchemist was draped across the room like a shroud. One day he would be forced to go in and seek it. For now, it was sufficient to be aware of that. Equally, he knew, time was not in infinite supply.

'Something is wrong with the wild roads,' he told himself again.

He turned and quickly descended all those stairs. Halfway down he thought he heard a voice calling him from a great distance. He stopped, lashed his tail and half turned back, though he was sure the voice hadn't come from above. It was so faint he couldn't tell who it was, yet so familiar it almost spoke its own name.

It was full of urgency.

PART ONE

Things Fall Apart

I

A Kindle of Kittens

The dog-fox known to his friends as Loves A Dustbin lay in the late-afternoon shade of some gorse bushes on top of a Cornish headland, waiting for his old friend Sealink to make up her mind.

Long-backed, reddish and brindled, he was strikingly handsome, until you saw that one of his flanks was completely grey, as if the fur there had somehow lost the will to retain its foxy hue. In another life, humans had shot him full of lead pellets: but for the support of his companions, his soul might have trickled away with the colour of his coat. Now two of that gentle but determined company were no more, and the rest had begun to scatter. After such dangerous events, after a lifetime's service in another species' cause, it was strange to lie here in the sunshine and be an ordinary fox again, bathed in the warmth of the returning spring, the confectionary scent of the gorse. He rested his head on his paws and settled down, prepared to wait as long as necessary. Patience was a luxury his other life had not encouraged. He intended to explore it to the full.

His mate, a vixen from the suburbs by the name of Francine, very good-looking and therefore disinclined to give and take, sighed boredly and said, 'Must we stay with her?'

'I promised Tag,' he answered simply. 'Anyway, she needs the company.'

After a moment he admitted, 'I know she's difficult to get on with.'

At this, the vixen sniffed primly. Loves A Dustbin contemplated her out of the side of his eye. She really was sodden mass of fur lining the shore as the tides pressed them gently but purposefully into the shingle. She had only been able to think:

Where was I when he needed my help? Somewhere out at sea, bobbing up and down on a boat with Pengelly and Old Smoky the fisherman. Fulfilling some damn ancient prophecy. Helping a foreign queen get to Tintagel Head and give safe and timely birth to the very kittens who were the cause of all this tragedy.

It had been difficult for her to mask her pain over these last weeks; but most of the time none of her companions had been watching her, anyway. They were all bursting with relief and optimism. They had, after all, defeated the Alchemist. A few domestic cats and a dog-fox had prevailed against appalling odds. They were still alive! They had new lives to make! Tag and Cy, reunited, chased and bit each other like youngsters. Ragnar Gustaffson, King of Cats, cornered whoever would listen and described in considerable detail his adventures on the wild road. Francine the vixen rubbed her head against Loves A Dustbin and promised him a life filled with Chinese take-away and sunlit parkland.

And as for the foreign queen's kittens –

One of them was the Golden Cat: one of them, when it grew up, would heal the whole hurt world. But who knew which of the three it was? No matter how hard she had stared at them, she hadn't been able to tell one from another. Tiny and blind-looking, they had pushed and suckled and mewed and struggled. They had all looked the same. Like any kittens she'd ever seen –

Like her own litter, in that other existence of hers, in another country, another world. I'm still alive, she thought. Perhaps they are, too. Her own kittens! In that moment, she knew that there was only one journey she could make now. The world could never be whole again; but she would damned well recover from it what she was owed. *We* make our lives, she thought. There ain't no magic: just teeth-gritting, head-down, eye-watering determination. She stood up slowly, but with a new resolve; stretched her neck, her

'None of you are very good at it yet.'

'She just wanted to get in first.'

'I did not.'

'You did.'

'I did not,' said Leonora. 'I'm bored with the mouse now,' she decided. 'It's rather small, isn't it?'

'You're just no good at hunting.'

Leonora looked hurt.

'I am.'

'You're not.'

'I bite your head,' said Leonora.

The kitten Isis stood a little apart and watched her brother and sister squabble, making sure to keep one eye on the place where the mouse had disappeared. Isis had her mother's eyes, dreamy and shrewd at the same time.

She suggested, 'Perhaps if we went round the back?'

The Mau blinked patiently in the sunlight. Her kittens perplexed her. They were already getting tall and leggy, quite fluid in their movements. They had no trace of their father's Nordic boxiness; and, if the truth were told, they didn't look much like Pertelot either. They had short dense fur of a mysterious, tawny colour. Every afternoon, in the long golden hours before sunset, the light seemed to concentrate in it, as if they were able to absorb the sunshine and thrive on it. 'What sort of cats are they?' she asked herself; and, unconsciously echoing her old friend Sealink, 'which of them will be the Golden Cat?' As they grew, the mystery, much like their colour, only deepened. Paradoxically, though, it was their less mysterious qualities that perplexed her most. The very moment of their birth had been so fraught with danger. The world had hung by a thread around them. Yet now –

Well just look at them, thought Pertelot a shade complacently: you couldn't ask for a healthier, more ordinary litter. Leonora, suiting actions to words, had got quite a lot of Odin's head in her mouth. Odin, though giving as good as he received, had a chewed appearance and was losing his temper. Claws would be out soon. The Mau shook herself.

'Stop that at once,' she ordered.

'Our brother is gone!'

If you had been in Tintagel town that early summer evening, you might have seen a large black cat half-asleep in a back street in a bar of sun. He was a wild-looking animal, robust and muscular, who weighed seventeen pounds in his winter coat, which had just now moulted enough to reveal stout, cobby legs and devastating paws. His nose was long and wide, and in profile resembled the noseguard of a Norman helmet. His eyes were electric, his battle scars various.

He was Ragnar Gustaffson Coeur de Lion: not merely a king among cats but the King of Cats. No-one went against him. His name was a legend along the wild roads, for mad feats and dour persistence in the face of odds. But he was a great-hearted creature, if a dangerous one. He exacted no tribute from his subjects. He gave more than he received. He was known to deal fairly and honestly with everyone he met, though his accent was a little strange.

Kittens loved him especially, and he loved them, pedigree or feral, sickly or well-set-up. He never allowed them to be sickly for long. One sweep of his great tongue was enough. He could heal as easily as he could maim. Toms and queens fetched their poorly children to him from all over town. There were no runts in Tintagel litters. There was barely a runny eye.

Everywhere Ragnar went, kittens followed him about with joy, imitating his rolling fighter's walk. Dignified sixteen-week-olds led the way. Tiny excited balls of fluff, barely able to toddle, came tumbling along behind. Slowly, like a huge ship, he would come to rest; then turn and study them, and muse with Scandinavian irony, 'They all can learn how to be kings from Ragnar Gustaffson – even the females!'

This evening, though, he dozed alone, huge paws twitching occasionally as in his dreams he toured the wild roads, bit a dog, retraced some epic journey in the face of serious winter conditions. Suddenly, his head went up. He had heard something on the ghost roads, something Over There. Seconds later, a highway opened three feet up in the children. In that well-planned zone between the wild and the tame, no-one wanted to kill foxes. Where Francine had tumbled and played as a cub, the risk was less death than photography. Even though the badgers, those untamed civil engineers, were threatening it all by undermining people's gardens and getting themselves a bad name, human beings were still out there every night with long lenses and photomultipliers. In cubs this bred a certain sense of security, on the heels of which often followed a demanding temperament and, paradoxically, a less than satisfactory life. Francine knew what she wanted, and though she was aware of death, her idea of nature had never given it much room. Nature was trimmed once a week. It featured fresh rinds of bacon, orange-flavoured yoghurt, a little spicy sausage. It had neither the addictive jungly glitter of the city, nor the *darkness* of the wild. Darkness never fell in the suburbs; and everything that was there one day was there the next day, too. You had to face things, of course, but nothing could be gained by dwelling on them. A steely will gave you the illusion of control.

As a result, Francine divided the world into the wild (nasty) and the tame (nice). Wild food – live prey, the sort you caught yourself – was nasty. The scraps left out for you on lawns were nice. The people who prepared food like that were nice. People were, on the whole, Francine believed, nice. They were civilized. On the other hand, the animal roads (being wild by definition) were uncivilized and nasty. The primal state was not something Francine aspired to. What she did aspire to, Sealink suspected, was matriarchy. Francine wanted Loves A Dustbin back on familiar ground, where she could encourage him to 'settle down'. She seemed an unlikely mate for him, given his dark history and adventurous life.

'I reckon he didn't have too much choice in the matter,' was Sealink's assessment. 'And once she's given him the cubs, he'll have even less. No more adventuring with cats.'

Particularly with cats like herself. Sealink had a distinct intuition that – as an attractive, intrepid and unencumbered female, albeit of an entirely different species – she was

Inside, shades of grey whirled and flowed, shadows upon shadows, as their muscles bunched and stretched, bunched and stretched and they ate the ancient ground away stride by giant stride.

Some time later – it seemed like hours, but how could you count time in a landscape without day and night, a world in which the sun shone through a haze, and the moon, shrouded by mist, hung always overhead? – Sealink could tell that they had covered a considerable distance. It was not just a sense of things shifting at speed, but also a feeling of enervation, of weariness achieved by long effort. And just as she had recognized the leading edge of this fatigue, a debilitating exhaustion crashed down upon her, sweeping through her like a cold, dark wave.

The calico shook herself. She could never remember having felt so tired, particularly on the Old Changing Way, which channelled all the energy of the world. It was as if a hand had reached up through the earth and squeezed her heart. She could hardly breathe. The foxes had stopped, too.

There was a voice, too, distant yet powerful, then the stench of something foetid. The voice seemed for a moment closer, and Sealink thought she heard the words, 'Got you!' Then the fabric of the wild road started to tear. Light from the ordinary world poured in like sand. The highway gave a great, galvanic convulsion, as if attempting to vomit, and suddenly Sealink and the foxes found themselves spun out of cold winds and icy plains into English woodland dappled with warm shade.

Sealink picked herself up and looked around.

'Damn! Ain't never been spit out like *that* before.'

Twenty yards away the foxes stood, blinking bemusedly in the sunlight, looking down at something which appeared to have fallen out of the wild road with them.

It lay on its side at the foot of a beech tree, and it was bigger, even in death, than Sealink in life. Despite experience with the wildlife of fourteen countries, she had never before encountered its shaggy grey coat or striped face. She thought briefly of the racoons of her native land. 'Your racoons, though,' she reminded herself, 'don't bulk

'But the Alchemist is dead. I saw him die. Him and the Majicou, both.'

The fox shrugged. 'There was always the chance that his magic would dominate the highways for a while. They'll be cleansed by use.' But he seemed unconvinced by this explanation. He had a fox's nose, and an understanding of the Old Changing Way second only to that of his original master. Old evil has a thin, faded reek; evil newly-done smells as pungent as dung. If anyone knew the difference between the two, it was Loves A Dustbin. 'Perhaps it's just some disease,' he said.

This caused Francine to step smartly away from the corpse.

'Oh dear! Come along now,' she advised. 'It's only something dead. We know these things happen, after all. We don't have to rub our noses in them every day.'

The next morning promised better things. Sunlight crept down through the ghostly breaths of mist in the river valley and burned them away to a sheen on the grass. Birds called in the ash trees. The light was pale and bright, so that everything looked brand-new, as if someone had come by in the night and retouched the reeds and butterbur, the broom and the jack-in-the-hedge, the golden celandines and wild thyme from a fresh palette of watercolours.

They came out onto heathland amongst lazy bees, and rabbits which bolted at the first scent of them, white scuts bobbing away over the close-bitten turf. Thwarted by the rabbits but fuelled by the warmth of the sun, the foxes took to play, ambushing one another from behind trees, chasing and biting each other's brushes.

After a while, Loves A Dustbin trotted back to the calico, his long red tongue lolling humorously out of his mouth.

'What a life, eh, Sealink? What a life!' He laughed wryly. 'Bet you never expected to see me acting like this. I never expected it myself. I thought my death was waiting for me behind every tree, watching in every shadow.' He chuckled. 'Ironic, isn't it? You think your life's over, and it's only just beginning.'

crawled under the skin and along the spine. Sealink leapt away from the wire in alarm.

'You do it!' she called to the dog-fox. 'You can dig, honey. You're damn near a dog, after all.'

Clouds of earth flew up from the fox's paws until finally the peg came free and the wire went slack. Francine opened pain-dulled eyes. Twitching the stricken leg, she found at last that she could flex the foot without the wire's terrible pulling. She sat up and started to lick at the hurt place, but even though the peg was out the snare was still biting deep into her flesh, invisible beneath fur and welling blood. They stared at the wound.

'Try and stand, babe,' Sealink urged, at the same time as Loves A Dustbin suggested, 'Now just lie there, and be still.'

They scowled at one another. The fox nosed at the snare. He touched it tentatively, but his nails were too big and blunt to get behind the wire. Sealink shouldered him out of the way. 'Leave this to Momma: she's got the proper equipment,' she asserted, and, bending her head to the wound, worked on it with a single razored claw until she had loosened it enough to get her teeth behind it. After that, it was like nipping a tangle out of fur: nip and lick, nip and lick, until her muzzle was a mask of red.

'I got to say, hon,' she told Francine, looking up with a ferocious grin, 'that I never expected fox blood to taste so *nasty*.'

The wire, released at last from its bed of flesh, lay like a coiled snake on the turf, a jewelled circle of red and silver, studded with little tufts of russet fur. Once the snare was off, Francine would let neither her mate nor the calico near her, or it. She snarled at them indiscriminately.

'I don't understand,' Loves A Dustbin said tiredly. 'She just won't part with it.'

'That ain't healthy, hon.'

It wasn't.

The wheezing of the vixen's breath through the night reminded Sealink of the sea breaking on a distant shingle wounded mate to see the silhouette of a large-furred cat staring down on him from the hillside above, its tail tip-curled and its ears flicking minutely. He could read the signs.

'Goodbye, Sealink,' he said softly. 'I hope you find what you're looking for out there.'

Francine whimpered at his feet. He bent his head to console her, and, when he looked up again, Sealink was gone.

visitors and lost children. Sometimes they would spend time with a fisherman's family, or in the steamy, scented fug of the Beach-O-Mat Laundrette, where the tabby would watch the clothes go round all day with a dreamy expression on her face. Her real name was Cy. Down at the quay, where she shamelessly courted the fishermen, they called her 'Trixie'. At this hour, Tag knew, she would be waiting for him in one of her favourite spots – a round granite building near the top of the hill.

Before these two adventurers turned up, no cat had entered that place. Not that they weren't curious. (A cat is a cat, after all.) Throughout the summer it was packed with human beings. They stood in lines then shuffled in. They shuffled round inside then shuffled out again, blinking and chattering in the sun. 'What do they do in there?' the village matrons would ask each other, giving their kittens a good spruce-up. 'With human beings it's so hard to tell, my love. Don't you find?' All a cat could say for sure was that it was a taller building than the chapel, more spacious than the lifeboat station. Its roof was home to some fat-looking gulls. Above the faded green doors an old enamel sign announced to the reading public:

OCEANARIUM.

Tag ran up the steps and slipped in through a gap low down between the two doors.

A single octagonal glass tank filled the echoing space inside. Whole shoals of mackerel scintillated there in millions of gallons of sea water, lorded over by thornback rays and spiny sharks. The sharks were powerful, streamlined, slim, less than two feet long. They circled endlessly. They pushed their clever noses out of the water and into the hot glare of the electric lamp which hung above their domain. All the creatures of the sea were represented. There were octopuses and squids. Lobsters made their homes in the detritus on the floor of the tank. Though the room itself was kept dark, a kind of ocean light – filtered through the sea water until it became a cool pale glow – illuminated the concrete floor between the tank and the walls, where just enough room of the tank, trailing a few bright motes and strings of matter. Cy watched it go, then turned and cuffed Tag's ears in delight. She rubbed her head against his. She purred.

'I got you a special dinner,' she said.

His heart sank.

From a niche at the base of the tank she withdrew one condensed-milk can (empty); one plastic clothes-peg; and two small fragile white shells. After some thought she added dry-roasted peanuts from the floor of an arcade, breadcrusts she had won off a herring-gull, and a square of milk chocolate still wrapped in blue silver paper. Tag thought he could probably eat the chocolate. He sorted through the rest with one paw and not much hope.

'Come on Jack,' she encouraged. 'Don't play with it. Get it down you!'

Then, before he could answer, 'If you liked that, you'll love this.'

With some ceremony she brought out her *chef-d'oeuvre* and dropped it in front of him. It was a cigarette butt.

'Very nice,' he said, as enthusiastically as he could. 'I think I'll leave that for after.'

The tabby pretended to groom herself. Then she sat back, eyes sparkling, head on one side. He realized she had been laughing at him all along.

'All right then,' he said. 'Where is it?'

She wriggled into the gap between the tank and the concrete floor until only her bottom showed; then, after some excited scrabbling about, backed out carefully and brought forth two pilchards. Their scales glittered. Their eyes goggled in the dim wash of light. They were plump and perfect (apart from the odd toothmark). They might still have been alive.

'Tag,' she said, 'we got stargazey pie!'

Though he loved her, Tag was suddenly a little tired. All the way home from the house by the river, he had felt he was being followed. In the tank a fish caught the light suddenly like sunshine on a coin, then vanished. An octopus hung high up against the glass as if pasted there, motionless but pulsing gently, waiting – even more patient and alien than ward. Then, as he turned towards the sea, there was a silent explosion over the beach, a split-second flare which faded instantly through all the colours of the spectrum to a black that was a kind of light in itself. Tag jumped to his feet. In the moment of illumination, he had seen the palms, the roiling surf, the wind whipping spray off the chop: and then a monstrous cat, which burst out of the naked air and began to forge its way in a kind of eerie slow motion across the beach towards him. Sand sprayed up from pads the size of dinner plates. Heat haze boiled round it. It came spilling the fire and anger of its life, waves of silent lightning, the ungrudging broadcast of substance into some space not quite the world we know. Its eyes were yellow. Its ears were flattened. Its great teeth gleamed white against a red mouth. Decreasing in size and speeding up as it approached, this fierce apparition hurtled up the three concrete steps from the beach. By the time it burst into the bus shelter, it was an ordinary cat: if you could ever use the word 'ordinary' of Ragnar Gustaffson Coeur de Lion, the New Black King.

'Ragnar!'

'Tag! Tag, my friend!'

Drenched and wild-looking, his fine coat disordered and dirty, Ragnar stood head down, sides heaving, filling the bus shelter with a kind of regal dejection. He was so exhausted he could barely stand. He was so anxious he could hardly speak.

'My friend! I— Tag, quick!'

'Ragnar, what is it?'

'Tag, something awful has happened!'

Tag left Cy in the bus shelter.

'I don't want you lost too,' he told her. She gave him a look, but he knew she would stay.

'Now run!' he said to Ragnar.

The tabby watched as they pounded over the sand and sprang one after the other into the ghost-ridden spaces of the wild road. Ten minutes later, Tag and Ragnar were stumbling around in the howling Tintagel dark.

'Odin!' they called as they went. 'Odin!'

'Pertelot—'

'It's not to try, Mercury. It's to find him. Do you see? You must, or how can I ever forgive myself?'

'We'll find him,' Tag promised.

What else could he say?

The two male cats quartered the headland, while the night battered them senseless with its cold wings. Merciless and unassuaged in the exposed corridors between the stands of gorse, the wind picked them up and threw them bodily about. Out there, they couldn't even be sure of one another's voices. Listen to that! A cat? A gull? The wind? Who knew? Worse, they often thought they could hear one another calling out, 'Tag! He's here!' or, 'Ragnar, Odin's safe!' Ghost voices, night voices, voices in the surf far below. A momentary trap for the heart, then disappointment. By sunrise they had to admit they'd found no sign – not a footprint, not a scuff-mark or a faint smell – of the missing kitten. They had combed rocks and ruins, they had teetered about on the cliff above the raging tide. They were soaked and shattered and their feet were sore.

Odin was gone.

The storm blew itself out with the dawn. The headland looked washed and emptied, all primrosey yellows and faint tawny browns. A single gull planed over the rocks at the edge of the cliff. Apologetic gusts of wind crept among the gorse stems. Later the sky would be very blue; for now, grey light like watered silk found out Pertelot Fitzwilliam, keening beneath her rock. Huge-eyed, Leo and Isis huddled close to her, but she was too distraught to comfort them. Tag and Ragnar, too tired to stand, told her what they now knew.

'We can't find him.'

'Go out again, then,' she said.

'When the light is better,' said Tag, 'we'll widen the search. When it's properly light I'll fetch some others.'

The Queen hissed at him.

'We have to rest now,' he said.

'I cannot rest,' said Ragnar.

The community there not comprising solely of the King and his family, there was plenty of help to be had. Among the ruins of the ancient castle, on the soil-creep terraces along the cliffs, in holes and under banks, lived many animals who had stayed behind after their part in the battle against the Alchemist. Foxes, badgers, urban feral cats settling down to find mates and found dynasties, even a pair of mink so angry no-one had yet dared to talk to them, now occupied the rising land eastward of the Head, or lived cheerfully in a muddle of warrens, fallen-down chicken coops and allotments at the edge of Tintagel town.

'Come and help,' Tag appealed.

'It took you long enough to ask,' they said.

Prey made peace – at least for the duration – with predator. Species that would only be seen dead with one another were spotted working the headland in teams – a rook with four young herring-gulls, the two mink with an old grey squirrel who called himself Broadsword. Cats co-operated with foxes to comb the town in case Odin had somehow made his way there and got lost. A very old race-horse named Smithfield went over the paddock fence every night just after dark and quartered the territory for twenty miles in every direction.

Nothing.

Two weeks passed, and then a third. Depression filled them all. Even the climate collaborated in this: a heatwave set in suddenly, and burned the grass brown. June brought an upsurge of human visitors to the ruins of the castle. They came from thousands of miles away, to wave their arms, blink in the sun and talk, talk, talk. They trudged along the complex contours on the northern flank of the peninsula, charmed and exhilarated by the way the land fell away in huge windy chamfers to the tide. Talk, talk, talk. (The *felidae* come here, of course: but more quietly. It is a place of pilgrimage for them, too. They remember how, in the Fourth Age of Cats, Atum-Ra and his Queen – who was also called Isis – arrived here from Egypt armed only with unborn kittens and the magic of warm countries, to reopen the old wild roads.) You had to keep out of their way. Their find Cy alone on the clifftop watching the sun go down under some long black clouds.

'Hello,' he said.

He licked the side of her face, where each short hair was tipped and ticked with tabby gold. All cats inhabit the tabby: or anyway they have hung up their coats there at some time or another. She tasted of wine. Flowers. Yolk of egg. She tasted of Cy.

'You're nice,' he said.

She seemed abstracted.

'Hi, sky pilot,' she said after a moment. 'Good day at the office?'

'I looked at spiders.'

'Fine. But see this?' she said. 'This is the story so far. I nearly died here, Jack. Remember? It was nip and tuck. I was spreadeagled on the Wheel of Flame. The Alchemist had burned me to the ground, you know?' She shivered. 'There was fire all round. But for the big Norwegian, I was going to cash my chips.' She shook her head. 'Oh, Tag, he seems so down now, that New Black King. I want to help him. And the kittens – I tell 'em things, but they don't stay to listen.'

'They hardly know where to turn,' said Tag. 'They miss their brother.'

They did miss him. But while Leo was clearly downcast, she knew what she wanted, and already had the air of a cat who could make decisions. (Though she kept them to herself, which did not help later.) Isis found it harder to live with loss.

In many ways, Isis was the most puzzling of the three kittens – quiet, clever, obedient, neat in her movements, but at the same time as unknowable as air. She evaded your understanding. The moon was her planet. She was drawn to water, to twilight, to all things that changed and shifted. The circumstances of her birth had been no stranger than that of her siblings: but Isis was open to the shadows. She had a drive to the invisible. She felt, she said, the strong dead awaiting their resurrection. They were curled up in every leaf. As a tiny kitten, she could already be found sitting and blinking and staring at unseen things – for her, every object enter St Madryn's by its primitive northern doorway. A wind had got up by then. The whole length of the graveyard stretched between them.

'Isis?' called Leo.

Isis looked round once. Her eyes flashed blank and empty. Then she was gone.

'Isis? Wait for me!'

Three hours later, just before dawn, Tag, Ragnar and Leo stood just inside St Madryn's – known to humans, who understand less of their own history than they think, as St Materiana's – looking down towards the east window, which had begun to harbour a faint but growing light. The whitewashed walls were tinged with pink and gold. Above, the complex roof-beams stretched away in the echoing silence; below, it was glossy pews. The air seemed to coil on itself, as if something had just that minute left the church.

Tag raised his head and sniffed. Polished wood. Flowers. Cold old stone.

Was there something else?

'Keep an eye open for rats,' he warned. 'This is just the sort of place you find them.'

'Show me a rat,' bragged Leo. 'That's all.'

She laughed.

'I won't treat it well,' she promised.

'Isis!' she called.

'Hush,' said Tag.

'Isis, I know you're in here!'

Her name was written on the air, they could listen to it with their noses. But why had she come here, and where was she now? The two adult cats stood shifting their paws uncomfortably on the tiled floor of the nave. They eyed the artefacts hanging on the walls. A kind of diffidence, an embarrassment on behalf of humankind, caused them to look away from the emblems carved into the reredos – spears and nails and whipping-posts. Leo, who felt no need to understand the things humans do, marched about, bellowing, 'Isis!'

Nothing.

Suddenly, dawn was upon them, in a soundless, unusual

penetrated the Head, the pipe widened, and fell away suddenly into a series of polished steps and ledges as rounded and complex as wax from a burning candle. It was a committing descent. Some of the steps were eight or ten feet high. 'How will we climb back up?' Tag thought. He decided not to ask Ragnar, who looked less than happy to be under the ground. Eventually, the going eased off. They found themselves in a wide, low passage, floored with crushed shells and tiny fibrous flakes of slate. A salt wind blew into their faces. A pale radiance seemed to spring from the damp, smooth walls. Leonora ran ahead, tail up, in little fits and starts, halting every so often to look back.

'That daughter,' grunted Ragnar. 'Where does she get the energy?'

'At least she's quiet now,' said Tag.

They listened appreciatively. Into the silence came a long, shooshing sound. Then another, like a breath.

'The sea,' said Ragnar.

'I imagine so.'

Ragnar looked apprehensive.

'Do you think the tide comes all the way in?'

'No,' said Tag decisively.

But he did.

The passage ended abruptly, on a ledge fifteen feet up the back of a great domed cave. Tag stared out. A smell of iodine and rot. Huge boulders, draped with fluorescent green weed which made them resemble velvet cushions in a sitting-room. They were surrounded by pools of old tide water. On the other side of the cave, so bright he could barely look into it, a slot of blue-white daylight, split into long beams by the intervening rocks. Against that light, he could just make out the lonely figure of Leonora, sitting at the entrance looking out. Her mouth was open, but all he could hear was the tide, crashing against the rocks at the base of the Head.

'How did she get down there?'

'Jumped, I should say.'

Tag looked at the nearest boulder. It was a long way down, and if you missed –

Tag stared. No kitten, not even the iron-willed Leonora Whitstand Merril, could survive that tide. He knew he could never face the Queen again, nor bear the expression on Ragnar Gustaffson's careworn face, if his friends lost their surviving child. Besides, he had always loved and admired Leo for a confidence he did not remember in himself at that age.

'Stay here!' he warned Ragnar.

He drew himself together. His head dipped once, twice, as he marked the place in all that fury he'd last seen Leonora. His hindquarters fidgeted and were still. A heartbeat pause. Then he unbent himself in an arc as bright as a rainbow.

The ocean boomed and coughed upon the rocks. It rose up to meet him. It was all round him, and there was no more Tag, only struggle and chaos and fear. He thought his heart would stop from the cold. The tide dragged him into its salty recesses, where it battered him, then flung him up, up, up again and out into the air. He was up in the air in a mist of spray! He felt the sun on him, he felt himself turn slowly over. He saw rocks, blue sky, a cliff with a puff of cloud above it, then sky and green brine again. He was sucked down to where the deep stones rolled around in the draw and backlash of the water – he heard their voices grind and growl against the fixed land – and there he found Leonora. A glimpse of her in a stinging salt-grey fog – bubbles came out of her gaping mouth – then they were whirled together like two rags in a washing-machine. He got her by the scruff, then lost her again. He clutched at her with his teeth, his front legs, his heart. 'Let me up now!' he told the water. But it only drew him further down between the stones. He felt them roll around him in blackness, huge slow grinding forms. He thought of the spiders in their frail webs. 'Hold on, Leonora!' he thought. His breath was a stone in him. He held on to her. He held on. He told the water, 'Let us up now!' But the water had them. One of Leonora's legs was caught between the rocks. The salt tide pulled at her. Nothing. Tag pulled at her. Nothing. Bubbles came out of her mouth. 'Leonora!' There was a dull booming all around: they were in the water for good, things were going from grey been constructed. An arrangement of pebbles, barnacle shells and bits of seaweed, it looked at first like an accident of the tide. Then you saw what it was meant to represent:

'Ha,' said Leo, who had regained her confidence. 'I thought as much.' She stood up on a boulder, stretched to her full length against the wall; and, failing to quite reach the symbol with her nose, dabbed at it with one paw. She fell off the boulder, jumped back up and tried again.

Ragnar gave her a look.

'There are times,' he told Tag, 'when a daughter – how can I say this? – is less of a blessing than I have imagined. But she is right.'

Tag pushed Leo out of the way and examined the symbol.

'The kittens may have been taken away by human agency,' was his opinion. 'But no human being made this. It smells of something else. It smells of – ' He shook his head, wishing for the nose of Loves A Dustbin, that organ so educated it could detect life in the dead. 'I don't know what it smells of,' he concluded. 'But humans didn't make it.'

'In which case,' Ragnar said, 'we should enquire, "If not humans, who?"'

'Who indeed?' the New Majicou asked himself darkly.

'They were taken by the sea,' Leonora insisted, in a determined effort to regain the attention of her elders.

She dropped to all fours, raised her head, and opened her mouth to allow damp, salty air across the exotic sensory organ – not quite smell, not quite taste – cats keep there. Suddenly, she was off again, this time towards the cave's landward entrance. The back wall barely gave her pause, though it slowed the two adult cats. They shrugged; exchanged a glance of reluctance; and did their best to follow. She scampered along the slate-floored passage, turned the 'staircase' by a series of deft leaps to intermediate grimly. 'I am the Majicou now. It is my responsibility. I will be back and forth, here and there. We may not see each other so often. To be safe, you should go north and live with Cy, and be looked after by our friends the fishermen.'

'We won't leave here.'

'But Pertelot – '

She gave him a look of reproach.

'And we will never live with human beings again. Mercury, how could you ask that?'

'Easily. Whoever took Odin and Isis will return for the third kitten. You know that. We are up to the tips of our ears in something here: I feel it.'

'Even so.'

Tag had always found her difficult to convince. He might be the Majicou: but she was the Mau. Though she had visited it only in dreams, another land spoke through her. Ancient responsibilities ran hot and mysterious in her veins. Also: he loved her too much to argue. When she sat up straight and powerful like that, and stared at him with her eyes half closed, he could only look away. He watched the fishing-boat as, bobbing like a silly painted cork, it rounded a distant dove-grey point, a headland barring its way as lazily as a human arm outflung across the water. Suddenly he had an idea.

'Then at least go to the oceanarium,' he said. 'It's empty at night. In the day you can – ' He paused. What could they do? Then he had it. 'In the day you can have a holiday,' he said.

'What's a holiday?' demanded Leonora.

'I'm not entirely sure,' said Tag. 'Human beings are doing it all the time.'

'Are there fish on a holiday?'

'More than you saw in your recent visit to the sea,' said her father. 'Don't interrupt when your mother is thinking.'

After a moment, the Queen blinked once.

'Very well,' she said.

Cy the tabby stood up, stretched briefly, then turned round and round in a delighted circle, tail up, rubbing her head against their heads in turn. A purr like the clatter of a

He paused. His gaze rested on them one by one, uncomfortable, intense.

He said again, 'Find me the golden kittens.'

The proxies fled. Tag followed them into the night, on a search of his own. He burned like a meteor in long flat arcs down the Old Changing Way. He was looking for Loves A Dustbin, who, as the original Majicou's lieutenant, had lived through more of the secret war against the Alchemist than anyone now alive. As he travelled, proxies came to him with their reports of nothing. Nothing to be heard. Nothing to be seen. Nothing to be found. 'If you can't do anything else, at least find me the dustbin fox,' he told them. 'Send him to me.' But the fox, it seemed, had gone to earth. Was that significant in itself? Towards dawn, Tag stumbled across a *vagus*, a scrap of the Old Life, in upland oakwoods somewhere north of the city, and, after two hours of mutual stalking, ambush and debate, despatched it back into the deep communal consciousness where it belonged. Finally, he returned to Cutting Lane. There, he dozed for a while with his eyes open.

Suddenly he thought, 'Unless it is Leonora, we have already lost the Golden Cat.'

answering, 'Just swanned right in before takeoff. A proper English lady.' And, when Sealink wriggled out of their arms and applied herself to the door again, 'She's cute, but a real nervous flyer.'

She was a hit with the passengers.

'Guess you can't throw her off now,' they told the cabin crew. 'Guess she got her free ride.' They said, 'Just make sure she doesn't open that damn door!' That had them all laughing.

Sealink, meanwhile, worked obsessively at the door, even though another voice in her head urged, 'Get a grip, hon.' She shredded the airline carpet. All the way over the grey ocean, she was a haunted cat: but, curiously enough, the sense of her kittens faded directly the airplane touched its wheels to the Moisant Field airstrip. Was that a good sign? Was it a bad one? She had no idea. She was on brand-new territory here, with nothing to go on but instinct. Ghost kittens, memories of kittens. They frazzled her when they were there; she missed them when they weren't. She wasn't used to this. What if none of it worked out?

'You'll find 'em.'

And, setting her chin high, she resolutely made her way across the tarmac, ignoring the trucks and carts, the aircraft groaning and complaining as they taxied from place to place, the human beings distracted and panicky as they dragged their baggage about. She was careful never to run. A *running cat catches the eye* was a saying she recalled from her own kittenhood, though since she had no more recollection of her mother than her name – Leonora Whitstand Merril – she guessed the advice came from one of the many scarred old tomcats she had once hung out with on the Moonwalk, the wooden boardwalk that ran along the banks of the great Mississippi river.

The Moonwalk! That promenade of soft airs and gently-riven dreams, whose denizens, though luckless and self-defeatingly individual, had always known how to live – how to eat, how to love, how to improve the midnight hour!

'I'm back,' she told them in her heart, as she skirted the glass-walled buildings of the terminal.

pixilated, banded-up with other runny-eyed disobedient brats – driven by the same mix of hormones and nosiness, all zest and gall and natural bristle, elated to find themselves out there unsupervised among all the scary grown-up cats – she had tumbled hourly down the curves and re-entrants to burst out at some unplanned destination with a puzzled 'Wha—?' and a prompt collapse into group hysteria, play-fighting and general bad behaviour.

'How'd we get here?'

'This here is a church, Octave! You brung us here to pray?'

'No, I brung you here to *prey*.'

Young queens, propelled into the flux by drives they barely comprehend, glory in its sustaining power, which – comprising partly as it does the souls of a million queens down the ages, all enjoying their new-found power – is primal and shared. To begin with, it had delighted Sealink to make the gift of her own individuality. It was fine to be feline! To walk out, tail up and boardwalk-bold, a cat among other cats, was enough. It had filled her with pride. Later she was not so sure. As her sense of self developed, her enjoyment of shared experience had declined. Was she some ordinary cat? Honey, she was not! She was the Delta Queen, good-looking, strong, daring, and – above all – unmistak-able. Tomcats pursued her. Other queens were jealous, their eyes hardened when she hove into view, hips rolling like a whole shipful of sex. She laughed in their faces and passed on by.

That was how she had made an adventure of travel on the more visible surfaces of the world. Cars, boats and planes, invited or not; on her own four feet if she had to, grinding out the miles to the next ride. How many human drivers, tired at the end of a long day, had rubbed their eyes at that ostrich feather of a tail and motored on, dismissing it as a hallucination? How many more, by truckstop and diner, not having an atom of shared language had understood its message nevertheless – 'Say, babe, you goin' to Topeka?' Crushed-shell lots, juke joints, sleep snatched in the back of some redneck pick-up rusted out to orange lace, so you fish in various stages of decay; the dry, musty scent of diseased pigeons; engine oil, human sweat, roasting pecans. Somewhere close by, someone was deep-frying shrimp popcorn. Oddly disoriented, Sealink closed her eyes, inhaling deeply. It smelled as much like home as anything could. And yet –

Familiar ground, brand-new territory.

There was a sudden eruption amongst the crates. A bit white cat, his face marked by long, gummy runnels down the nose, burst from the debris, scattering chewed corn husks, sad crusts of bread and bits of rotting tomato. His shoulders were wide and muscled, his haunches bunched ready to spring. A new pink scar showed raw against the fur of his lower belly. An onion skin hung out of his mouth. Why was he eating this crap? Sealink stared at him with a kind of puzzled distaste. On the other hand, you had to begin somewhere.

'I was looking for some kittens,' she said.

She might not have spoken. The white cat hissed. His ears – such as they were – went flat against his skull. Unsavoury curses spilled out of his mouth.

'This is my food,' he said.

Sealink was disgusted. It was not what she had expected. It was not your hometown welcome-back. It was not the voice of the Big Easy. 'This ain't food,' she said, treating their surroundings to a look of contempt. 'It ain't even consumer-quality garbage.' She decided on a change of tack. 'Look, babe,' she went on, in the drawling contralto which had served her well in fourteen countries – a voice which had charmed *camels*, let alone tomcats (whose knees it had been known to turn to jelly) – 'let's take it easy here—'

'This is all mine,' said the white cat. He put his head down and began to advance on her.

'OK,' she told herself. 'So the voice didn't work.'

She thought, 'Time for plan B.'

Unsheathing her claws, which she kept impeccably honed, she hurled herself at the white cat. He was some pounds heavier, and his muzzle was scarred with the marks of many previous encounters. But, as he lunged to meet her, mothered litter after litter of scrawny kittens, extending her court from the Riverwalk to Esplanade. When the moon was high over the Mississippi, the levee had echoed to her ear-splitting yowls. Toms had traipsed from far and wide to visit the famous Kiki, then left the next day, scratched and sore, with a tale to tell of a wild Creole queen with a misleading name and insatiable appetite.

This was probably yet another of her myriad offspring.

'Since when does any cat need Kiki La Doucette's permission to come down the Grand Highway?'

'You not bowed your head to La Mère, you better vamos.'

Sealink was infuriated. So much for shared heritage! She'd travelled half the world for this? To be set upon by a flea-bitten tom with the manners of a hound dog was bad enough; but to be expected to pander to some raddled old yellow queen who'd once tried to scratch her eyes out? Not likely. She turned her back with calculated disdain upon the tortie-and-white, stuck her tail straight up in the air like a standard-bearer marching to war, and sway-hipped it down the alley. Without looking back, she called, 'I don't bow my head to anyone, sweetie; you go tell your mama her old friend the Delta Queen is back in town.'

The little tortoiseshell cat watched Sealink turn the corner left towards the streetcar tracks and the river. There was a strange light in her eye. When the calico had disappeared from view she stood up, shook out each leg in turn, muttered something in a singsong voice and slipped into a tributary highway. Three or four large blue flies rose as if out of the ground to buzz lazily around the fruit crates.

Everybody who is looking for something in New Orleans is bound to end up on the boardwalk. Down there, at least, everything was much as Sealink remembered. The Mississippi stretched away grey and leaden to the distant greenery on the opposite bank. Over at the Algiers docks, cranes towered above the water like huge predatory birds. She crossed the wooden planking and jumped down onto shrimp and crab and mudbugs. As if from nowhere cats would appear in droves, a purring, mewing entourage who would wind themselves adoringly around his feet until all the food was gone, when they would slip away in selfish bliss amongst the shadows, or drift along the weedy shore-line to groom and doze. To Sealink, Henry had seemed perfect. He smelled wonderful – fishy and catty and hardly human at all. Other people avoided him. He never tried to pick cats up, never forced his will upon them, but arrived, uncomplaining and punctual, every night to smile upon their impersonal and mercenary greed.

She rubbed her cheek against the bench. It smelled disused. There were crumbs under the seat, gone hard and stale.

Not even the pigeons were hanging out here any more.

She moved south towards the Toulouse Street Wharf, still on the lookout for the denizens of the levee, until struck by a scent that made her nose twitch. The further down the boardwalk, the stronger the smell became. Sealink sniffed appreciatively. An enormous sense of well-being swept over her. There is little in life quite so fine as those moments a hungry cat experiences immediately in advance of satisfying its appetite. Her nose led her to a trash can at the end of the boardwalk. It was an undignified squeeze for a cat of her size, but was dignity at issue? It was not. Sealink squirmed her way into the trash like a furry bulldozer and emerged some seconds later with her jaws clamped around a chicken carcass which was still transmitting its irresistible signals into the humid Louisiana air. To Sealink, these were signals of love. She slipped with a grace born of many years of patient scavenging back onto the boardwalk. There, she wedged the deceased fowl against a fence-post and, after some awkward manoeuvring, managed to insert her entire head inside it. There were bits of gizzard left!

Thus engaged, she did not notice the large ginger cat that had been sitting silently for some time on top of the fence slip soft-footed to the ground behind her. The tabby mark-ings of his coat swirled like a great, furry magnetic field in

The marmalade cat stretched out his neck, cleared his bitten throat, looked shifty.

'Well, honey, it sure looked like a invitation to me.'

Sealink growled.

'How could any red-blooded male resist? What could be more alluring than the sight of such a fine, mature queen offerin' herself like that?'

Sealink gave him a hard stare. He looked back at her and the lazy eye in the middle of the black spot drooped, so that for a moment Sealink thought he had winked. She felt the short fur on the top of her head bristle.

Suddenly she thought, 'Why, he ain't but a boy,' and laughed.

'Honey, I was eatin'! I wasn't offerin' myself, to you or any male. And I don't take too kindly to bein' called old, either.'

The tomcat, embarrassed, set about an elaborate toilette, starting with his face and front paws.

'So what's your name?' she asked at last.

'Red.'

'Figures.'

'And where do you call home, babe?' she enquired.

'This burgh is where I first seen the light of day,' Red explained. 'But foreign places have not been foreign to me, I confess; and though I return here every so often, home is just 'bout anywhere I lay my head.' And indeed, despite his Southern drawl, he had a smell the calico recognized. It was the smell of docks and truckstops, cardinal points on the long, genial road to nowhere. 'My story's easy told. I've been places where the nights are sweet with lilac, and places not so sweet. I'm a cat you don't meet every day, a cat of no fixed abode – ' he gave her a look that had already shattered a heart or two along the way ' – and I like it like that.'

Sealink smiled into her fur at this callow Delta spiel, culled from the monologues of the travelling toms Red had met on his journey: it was one she had rehearsed a time or two. She warmed towards him in consequence, and found herself saying, 'I know that feelin'. I'm from just about anyplace myself.'

IV

The Laboratory

The cat known only as Animal X passed his time with four other cats, in a five-chambered metal cabinet which left only their heads free to move. There were other cabinets nearby – though Animal X couldn't see them – and other cats in those cabinets. Some of them had been afraid when they were first brought here. Some of them had been angry. Now they accepted their situation. The only thing they couldn't get used to was not having enough mobility to groom themselves. The strain of this left them dull-eyed. Their necks were chafed into sores by the enamelled edge of the cabinet. In an attempt to relieve the irritation this caused, they stared outwards away from each other all day while human beings came and went around them, treating them as if they weren't there and saying things like, 'Hanson wants the work-ups as of yesterday, but he won't say why.' Or, 'We can do the blood now, on its own, but it won't show anything. Doesn't he know that?' These people never touched the cats in the cabinets. They didn't need to.

'Doesn't he know that?'

Of all the things the human beings said this interested Animal X the most, because he knew so little.

He had no idea who he was. He certainly didn't know himself by the label Animal X. The life he lived did not require anyone to call him anything. It only required him – so he supposed – to feel pain. He woke up and he was in pain; he was in pain and then he slept. Something had been done to him. He felt a fool at having to stand there in one place all day, he felt as if it was his own fault. 'Somehow I got caught,' he would tell himself. He smelled his own smell suddenly, and a kind of shame went through him. He was slowly losing their shape and coherence. And, whatever else he thought, he had no doubt that the words, and the light – especially the light – reminded him of some other life he had once lived. Things stirred and flickered just out of sight at the back of his mind. He couldn't remember what he was remembering: but whatever it was had been part of a more comfortable existence – any rate, a more interesting one. These fragments of memory made him both happy and inexpressibly sad.

On a good day Animal X could just see, out of the very corner of his eye, the heads of the nearest cats to him in the cabinet. (A better view could be had by turning his head, but if he did that he was given a sharp reminder of the sore that went round his neck like a collar.) Next to him on his right was a cat so depressed it never spoke. This cat had replaced a very lively female, dimly but fondly remembered by Animal X as 'Dancey'. (Dancey – Animal D – had never stopped talking. Everything she said began with the announcement, 'As soon as I get out of here – ') On his left was Stilton, Animal B. He liked Stilton and the silent cat. Living so close, they were important to him. If they smelled a bit strongly, it was a smell to wake up to, a dependable smell. If there was something odd about the shape of their heads, well, something had been done to all the cats here, and perhaps there was something wrong with the shape of Animal X's head too.

Stilton had been in the cabinet longer than any of the others. He predated both Dancey, whose departure Animal X had witnessed, and 'the Longhair', a cat Dancey herself had often remembered fondly. Stilton had got his name because he always talked about Stilton cheese. He would stare into space for a bit and then say, as if he was continuing a conversation that had already started, 'Now, what you can get if you go to the factory shop (well, what my owners used to get anyway), is seconds. A bit overripe perhaps, you see. A bit runny. So for seventy pence you can get this great wheel, this whole cheese. It's a lot, but they'd split it with their friends. I'd seem them eat it after their before the cabinet? Can you?' Neither of them could, although they tried hard enough. After all, they were cats: they knew how to persevere. They tried so hard that, in the end, they were making up stories about themselves. They tried out memories the way a human being tries on clothes, picking them up and then putting them down apparently at random.

'I was a town cat, me. Oh yes. It was back yards every night, back yards and singing and bad sisters, out on top of the wall where everyone could see. It was one long party for us, and no regrets!' Then, after a pause, 'I've got a bit of a funny neck now, but I've got no regrets.' Next night, the same cat would be claiming, 'Sometimes I think I must have lived on a farm. You know? Because I remember the smell of straw, and the warm breath of the cows.'

'You remember that, do you?'

'I do. Sometimes I think I do remember that.'

So their bemused dialogue droned on into the night, thoughtless and obsessive, broken by longer and longer pauses, until near dawn it petered out.

'Can you see what colour I am? I've got this feeling I was a tortoiseshell.'

By then, though, Animal X was asleep.

Sometimes he believed he had had another life than this one, sometimes not. One thing was clear: when he tried to remember the things that happened to him before he came here, his head hurt even more. Generally, he accepted that his life now would always be pain.

Plenty went on in the room, even if you could only see directly forward from your cabinet. There was a white door with a small square of glass in it, and people came in and out through that at most times of the day, though rarely at night. They were always talking. With a sigh and a shake of the head: 'Figures that simply don't mean anything unless they're backed by observation.' And then: 'I know he said that. But look at his track record.' They all had the same white coat on, but each one had a different smell, and their shoes creaked on the polished wooden floor. Animal X clearly a kitten. Yet, despite its leggy, slightly unformed lines and immaturity of face, it was bigger than many a full-grown tom – he had never seen a kitten so big. Before he could decide anything, it had vanished. But he was to see more of it, almost immediately. They had difficulty getting it out of its cage. And then, while they were trying to transfer it to a cabinet, it escaped.

Much of this took place behind Animal X's head. All he heard were shouts from the human beings – 'Look out, just pull it out of there, can't you?' 'I've got it, I've got it, it's OK.' 'Bugger!' – and a bubbling, ululating wail which rose suddenly into the fine mad high-pitched shriek of outrage all those confined cats remembered so well. Then the new animal streaked into view, low to the ground, ears flat, eyes bulging. It stopped for an instant in front of Animal X's cabinet to gaze back over its shoulder at the pursuit. It was a male kitten, all anger and beauty, piss and vinegar, but Animal X could see how much fear was mingled with its rage. 'Hide now,' he heard himself advise quietly. 'You can get out later, when one of them opens the door.' He was immediately aware what a counsel of despair that was. Sides heaving, hindquarters dropped protectively, every muscle bunched and hard under the short, velvety coat, body rocking to the beat of its own heart, the kitten stared up at him with a kind of empty defiance. For a moment he thought it would acknowledge him, tell him contemptu-ously, 'I'll never be trapped like you.' Instead it spun round and rushed away, to be followed an instant later by three or four human beings, all hands and shoes and spectacles. Their huge dull faces red and sweating, they grunted and stumbled after the escapee; while, unknown to them, the cabinet cats cheered it on. 'Go on,' they called. 'Go on!'

That kitten had come into their lives from nowhere, and passed in half a minute from a zero to a legend. Hopes they never knew they had were invested in him. When he hid, they looked away, in case his pursuers should follow their line of sight. When he upped and ran, their feet scrabbled and scratched uselessly in the cabinets. They were trying to run on his behalf, and at the same time catch for themselves

The glorious savage, brought to bay in a corner by the cupboard, suddenly became silent and passive and was taken away, dangling at arm's length like the empty pelt of a cat, out of Animal X's sight.

There was a shocked and empty pause in the cabinets.

Then someone whispered, 'Did you see the eyes on him? Weird!' And someone added, 'He was something to catch, that one.' And someone else said, 'It's a shame.'

Suddenly, full of excitement, they all began to talk at once, shouting from cabinet to cabinet across the white room of their captivity, brought together in a way they had never been before. Animal X said nothing. He was saddened by this proof that life is, indeed, only capture, silence and the cage: only pain.

For some days afterwards the laboratory was quiet. Things went back to normal. The sunshine moved across the white wall, beginning a little earlier every day, lasting a fraction longer. No-one seemed to know which cabinet the gallant kitten had ended up in, if it had ended up in a cabinet at all. There were those that whispered it had not; they hinted at worse. As this rumour spread, conversation between the cabinets died out. Their occupants shrugged to themselves and went back to the long haul. Wall of Death – who had said nothing more anyway – became again the Silent Cat and stared ahead of himself all day. The human beings, perhaps, had received a reminder. They were a little more wary of their charges; but there was no more or less dried food in the stainless steel feeders than usual. The cats were fed last thing, just before the staff left, so that every evening the room was full of a sound like stones being sorted in a tin. Animal X regarded listlessly this manufactured stuff, with its strong but somehow unappetizing smell of fish products, and then, as usual, ate half of it.

'Sometimes,' Stilton told him as they ate, 'we'd have a nice bit of blue. That's a mould of course, they get the cheese like that by encouraging a mould to grow in it.'

'I think they've encouraged a mould to grow in this,' said Animal X.

burned and burned, then ignited in a great soft roar. A green flame exploded beneath the ceiling, spread rapidly, roiled down and across the laboratory floor. Everything in its path caught fire. Everything it touched was engulfed. Everything in the room began to fly apart, in complete silence. The cabinets were pulled to pieces and thrown about; equipment toppled through the burning air; the very walls tumbled outwards and away, pulled and twisted, as they went, into dust and detritus and falling bricks.

Animal X heard a voice say, 'Even this.' All the air was sucked out of him and he too was whirled away. He went end over end through the sky – forelegs splayed in front of him, feet spread, claws out as if they could find purchase on the air to slow him down – and landed in a vague, unending dream of kittenhood. He was very young. His mother was close. His brothers and sisters tottered and fought around her. They bounced and sprang. They were so safe! surrounded by something that stretched away in all directions and yet cupped them like a hand. He could feel it. Was it love? What was it? It cupped Animal X too tight, and everything he knew was taken away.

When he woke again, he was chilled right through. His fur was wet. The light was grey. He opened his eyes and the first thing he saw was the laboratory door. Something was wrong with it. It was hanging off one hinge, leaning into the room like a drunken man into an alley. He stared for a moment, then, not yet able to understand quite what he was seeing, let his gaze be drawn away. The laboratory had been opened up in a dozen other places. The windows had blown out, the ceiling had sagged and split. Loops of cable hung down. The floor was thick with splinters of wood and shards of glass, the air with plaster-dust through which fell a fine cold rain. The examination table, site of so many indignities and so much pain, lay buckled and barely recognizable at the foot of a wall. It looked as if it had been thrown there by some enormous angry hand, which had gone on without a pause to dissect every cabinet into its component panels. Barely damaged, these lay distributed to lick one another clean, but their bodies were so relieved to feel the touch of another cat again that they fell asleep immediately. They stayed that way for much of the morning, unwilling to leave the site of their old cabinet – though they kept a distance between themselves and the bodies of the cats they had shared it with. Animal X found himself remembering those three with more affection and less discomfort than he had expected. 'The Silent Cat had given up speaking because he didn't have anything left to say about life,' he thought. 'Death must have been a release for him.' Then he reminded himself, 'I never knew the others, though I heard them talk. They might have been interesting cats.' He thought, 'I would have known them better if they'd been next to me in the cabinet.' His memory was already garbled and confused, so that some repeated phrase of theirs had become mixed up with the luminous dawns, the rattle of hard food in a tin tray, the flutter of paper on the cork board by the door. It all seemed one, and surprisingly like a life.

The rain stopped. The sun came out. Mid-afternoon saw the two survivors poking about independently in the ruins.

Cabinet life had so wasted them that they had to teach themselves to walk again. Animal X's progress was punctuated by unexpected skips and jumps, sudden shies and spasms of his depleted nervous system as it readjusted to the proper life of a cat. At first he felt rather excited by these sensations; but it was a vigour that proved illusory. He hadn't eaten since the previous evening. Despite his excitement, despite the optimism the watery sunshine had brought with it, he had no stamina, no condition, no muscles worth speaking of. Stilton was worse. He limped. His fur, draggled into hard, crusted little curls, tasted of blood when you tried to groom him. There was something pushed-in about his ribs. Sometimes he forgot where he was and stood swaying and blinking and repeating quietly, 'Now, my owners, you see – '

Once he called over to Animal X, 'Aren't we a pair, eh? What a pair!'

V

Leave it to Leonora

Tag sat on a shelf in the abandoned pet shop at Cutting Lane.

It was the end of a wet afternoon, and the light was fading to brown the other side of the dirty, rain-streaked windows. Soon, the street outside would echo briefly to the sound of hundreds of human feet. The sodium lamps would turn it orange. Then the noise would die away, and the pavements would belong to cats again. 'The night,' his old mentor had once advised him, 'is always the best time for doing the work of the Majicou.' So – though he could have done that kind of work at any time from Cutting Lane, so central was it in the web of the wild roads – Tag sat on his shelf to wait.

'Come on, night,' he thought.

As soon as he had finished here, he planned to visit a pie stall three streets away and eat battered scallops, white pudding. In the meantime he got up, shook himself, and was just turning round to find a more comfortable position when he heard a noise at the back of the shop.

Scrape.

It was like claws on bare wood. He heard it once and then again. 'What's this?' he thought. Scrape. Click. Scrape. Like a lame animal circling quietly in the back room.

Something had come along the wild roads to him, something that owed allegiance to the original master of Cutting Lane. Tag got to his feet and backed carefully along the shelf until he was hidden behind some thick spiderwebs. With no-one to teach him how to be the Majicou, he had learned caution early. Most of the proxies were harmless. Some weren't. He never showed himself until he was sure.

71

larger roads. Tag stood in the smell of mud and stared at the heap of corpses the dog had brought him to see. There were ten or fifteen of them. They were all cats. Their fur was sodden. Their limbs were entangled as if they had fought panickily with one another at the last. Their eyes bulged so hard that the whites showed. They had died with their ears back.

'How did this happen?' said Tag.

The dog looked at him dully.

'The life has been drained out of them,' it said. 'Something is wrong with the Old Changing Way. I don't know what.'

'Go away and learn more.'

'You are not the Majicou,' grumbled the dog.

'I am the New Majicou. Always come to me when you find something.'

'Yet there is no reward.'

'Find me two golden kittens and we'll see.'

The dog turned away with a sigh and dragged itself up the shingle towards the buildings. Something made it stop and say, 'I am a dog. A dog has a sense of smell. If I did not know better I would say I smelled the Alchemist on that road: I would not use it if I were you.'

Too late.

The New Majicou had gingerly negotiated the heap of dead cats and stuck his head in the highway.

What he found there was not unusual. How can a road go in all directions at once? No-one knows the answer to that. The Old Changing Way, which will take you anywhere in hardly any time at all, is full of ghosts. Nothing more can be said. Unless you know what you are doing it is a dangerous place to be. Even at the best of times.

'Hmm,' thought Tag.

He thought, 'Nothing here.'

But as soon as he pushed his way inside he knew that the old dog had been right. It was like moving through glue. He was exhausted suddenly, and his bones felt hollow. Worse, something was waiting for him. He couldn't say how he

'Hello, Tag,' she said shyly. Then she caught sight of the corpses.

He took her home immediately, and all the long, long way without a word spoken, so that her parents could scold her roundly in the dim green light of the oceanarium.

'What were you thinking of?' demanded the Mau. 'What could you have been thinking of?' While Ragnar Gustaffson shook his head and – conveniently forgetting his own first acquaintance with the Old Changing Way – said that in his opinion it was a very irresponsible thing, to travel wild roads as a kitten without protection or preparation.

'A very irresponsible thing, Leonora.'

Leo looked abashed for a moment. Then her confidence returned.

'I want my brother and sister back,' she said.

'We all want that,' said the Mau tiredly. 'You could help by not being taken in your turn.' With a kind of puzzled distaste she looked up at the great tank, where the sharks circled relentlessly in the illuminated water. 'We live here with these – ' for a moment she seemed lost for words ' – these fishes, to keep you safe.'

This only made Leo angry.

'I don't want to be safe,' she said.

She said, 'No-one is doing anything!'

'I'm doing what I can, Leo,' said Tag. Now that his fur had settled down, he felt mainly relief that he hadn't hurt her. Nor could he forget her expression when she saw the grotesque and pathetic heap of fur at the end of the highway. It was hard to stay angry, though Leo seemed to have no difficulty with that. 'I might have killed you by the river,' he added quietly. 'I had no idea who you were.'

She looked away.

'I'm sorry,' she said. He could see that she was, but that it wouldn't change things for now. He felt uncomfortable on her behalf – though he knew she wouldn't thank him for that either – as she turned and stalked off towards the door.

'Where are you going?' demanded the Mau.

'All these fish make me hungry,' said Leonora. 'I'm going

She added matter-of-factly, 'Mother dreams o[f]
times. She dreams almost every night.' Sh[e]
a moment. 'One day,' she said with a kind o[f]
[hau]teur, 'I shall dream of elephants too.'

[cont]inued to stare at her. He wondered if he had bee[n]
[compa]rable at her age. 'I only know that he can read,[']
['Would you call someone Elephant because h[e]

[can] reading?'
[was]n't entirely certain about that, either.
[We'll] see,' he said.
[He] knew what Uroum Bashou had told him: tha[t]
[humans] kept what they called 'books', and that the[y]
[A c]at was able to sense the meaning of the 'words[']
[boo]ks contained by passing his paw quickly along
[of] the text; or sometimes by licking it; or even by
[his] whiskers to sense faint changes in pressure caused
[mo]vement of the air across the print. Uroum Bashou
[close]d his eyes now that he had grown older – although
[...]that was how he had learned to read as a kitten,
[on] his owner's shoulder as his owner turned the
[... of] some interesting volume – *Birds of the Green*
[...] *Small Rodents of the Northern World: Their*

[... tir]ed of waiting and seeing,' said Leonora. 'Actually.'
[For a] moment, Tag looked amused.
[...yo]u actually are, are you?' he said. He jumped to his
[... wit]h an empty-eyed suddenness that startled her,
[... snapped] at a passing bee, and went bounding across the
[... sc]attering last year's leaves as he went. 'Then try and
[catch m]e if you can!' he called over his shoulder; and, with
[... van]ished.

[She ca]ught a twist of light in the corner of her eye, dived
[into the] highway before it closed after him. The world
[went s]ideways, righted itself, ghosts streamed past, the
[cold]s wind howled around her. She could see Tag in the
[...]distance, running tirelessly along in a kind of slow
[...] Echoes flew up from his pads in the shape of small
[...] birds. 'Call yourself a cat?' he taunted. And without

His main argument to Ragnar and Pertelot had been simple: 'If you forbid her she'll just keep doing it anyway.' They had seen the force of this. They had expected him to make promises, of course. Leonora must agree to do what she was told. She must always stay by him. Once all that was sorted out, he had tried to calm their fears further by adding, 'She'll soon get bored when she sees how humdrum it all is.'

'Don't misjudge Leonora,' the Queen had advised him grimly. Hurt feelings or not (and who could use such a phrase to describe the wells of sorrow and anger, the Egyptian deeps of the Mau's affections?), she loved her daughter. 'She's an untapped soul.'

In a way, both of them turned out to be right.

Leonora was soon bored.

'Love the world, Leo,' Tag would advise her. 'That's the secret of success. Love the world and follow your nose.' This axiom gave rise less to a search of the wild roads than a communion with them, less an interrogation of their denizens than a conversation. It hardly suited the Leonine temperament. True, she enjoyed learning how to find and navigate her chosen highway, how to recognize a safe or a difficult entrance, how to read the ever-changing smoky light. It was an adventure. 'Quick now, Leonora!' Tag would urge. 'Follow close!' Or, 'Wait! Wait here and make no sound!' She soon learned to listen for that edge in his voice, that promise of excitement and danger. And she soon fell in love with the bizarre and eccentric animals he knew – the 'creatures of Majicou' who had acted as agents, informants, proxies to the original guardian of the wild roads. She loved the marginal places they lived in, and the odd relationships they seemed to have with each other or with human beings. All this was rather exciting. But it was broken up by long periods at Cutting Lane, during which her teacher sat among the spiderwebs and seemed to do nothing at all.

Instead of changing his plan when it produced no discernible results, Tag only became thoughtful. On their third day along the Old Changing Way, he took her to some warning he turned at right angles into the wall of the world and vanished again. Leonora stood among the echoes, panting. 'What now?' she thought. 'What now?' the echoes said, as they fluttered round her muzzle. 'Oh go away!' she told them. Off she went again, and this time caught up with him a little sooner. 'I do call myself a cat!' she said; but he answered, 'Do you indeed? Then you already know the way. Such a clever animal doesn't need any lessons,' and disappeared again. So it went, from the huge ancient highways laid down by sabre-tooths after the ice receded, to the little local mazes made by domestic cats, Tag always ahead, always allowing her to catch up, until she was thoroughly out of breath and out of temper, and they stood in the cluttered yard of an abandoned red brick house somewhere in the Midlands, where early-evening light lay in slanting gold bars against the boarded-up windows, the scuffed and sun-bleached back door.

Into the door was set an old-fashioned wooden cat flap, scratched and battered and grubby with the passage of many cats. Above that, a smaller hole had been gouged in the door itself, perhaps so that the occupants could look out without themselves being seen. Behind the door, the air was disturbed by a stealthy movement, and a rank smell. One amber eye appeared in the hole and stared out at Tag and Leo. Its surface had an oily iridescence. Its pupil was dilated.

Leo rubbed her head nervously along the side of Tag's head. 'Is it Uroum Bashou?' she whispered.

'Go away,' said the animal behind the door.

'No,' said Tag to Leo. 'It is his guardian, Kater Murr.'

'Go away,' said Kater Murr again. Its voice was reasonable and dangerous. Its breath was bad.

'I am the Majicou,' Tag said. 'You know me, Kater Murr.'

'I know no-one.'

The amber eye was removed suddenly. Leo had a sense of something ponderous and ill-favoured shifting its weight in the gloom.

'Kater Murr, let us in,' said Tag patiently.

A contemptuous laugh came from behind the door.

walls had quietly sprung to life behind her as she passed.

She was unprepared for the top of the house – where everything had been knocked into one huge room, now lighted by the dull gold-and-orange wash of a setting sun, which ran like hot metal through a series of skylights and onto the scene below – or for the animal who greeted them there.

Uroum Bashou had once danced and scampered in the alleys of Morocco – or so he claimed. Now he lived in some state, albeit in the cold north, and books surrounded him. Books large and small, books bound with green and brown leather or orange paper, books in drifts, books in rafts. Closed books, open books, books swooning into piles, books whose wings and backs seemed broken. Books had slipped from the walls and slithered across the floors like the moraines left behind by some strange retreating glacier from a vanished age of print. Among them, like a pasha on a cushion on a souk, sprawled the Reading Cat, a browny-black, short-haired, skinny, long-legged old thing, who nevertheless exuded the dignity of the expert, the confidence of the emeritus professor. The fur around his ears was threadbare, as if he was a toy from the little sharp head of which someone had thoughtlessly rubbed the velvet. His eyes, a dim amber, were flecked with the many things he knew. When he spoke, though, his voice was light and fluting, the voice of a eunuch like a musical instrument in a closed courtyard; and he often spoke of himself in the third person.

When he saw Leonora, he began to purr.

'Uroum Bashou,' he greeted her, 'welcomes you, my dear. How can he help?'

'We are looking for two kittens—' Tag began.

Uroum Bashou ignored him.

'I see,' he said to Leonora, 'that you are admiring the Tail of Uroum Bashou.'

She was indeed looking at it, but not perhaps with admiration. It was as skinny as he was, and there was something wrong with the tip of it.

'Come closer. This is the story. In brief, a cat is born, a cat

83

'As ever.'

' – as ever. But the wild roads . . . The wild roads are uncomfortable, Uroum Bashou. They have begun to take where they should give. One day they are reliable, the next day they are not. Something is out of joint.'

Uroum Bashou nodded his little threadbare head.

'You walk wild roads,' he acknowledged, 'while the Elephant stays among his books: that is good. What does the Elephant know? This: there is more than one prophecy that speaks of a Golden Cat. This: the Golden Cat may not be what it seems. This: the Golden Cat may not be all of it, or the end of it. Do you see? I see that you don't. And yet: there is a fuse burning in the world today. I do not know who lit it, or how. But something quite new is coming, and not just to us cats.'

Leonora inspected one of her front paws modestly.

'I have often thought *I* might be the Golden Cat,' she suggested.

Their heads went up, and they stared at her for a moment or two; then they went back to their talk.

'Don't mind me, I'm sure,' said Leonora.

She reminded Uroum Bashou, 'It must be one of us, you know.'

But he only said, 'I believe all this began in Egypt, where we began the fatal relationship with men. Whatever happens will be one end of a great arc across the history of cats and human beings.' And he urged Tag, 'Don't let yourself be diverted, as I believe your predecessor to have been, by simple oppositions. If the world is to be made new, the Golden Cat must be more than some simple piece of magic. To heal the world it must do more than cure the ills of cats, or settle their old scores.' It was advice he had given before.

They spoke of such generalities for a moment, then Tag said, 'This is no longer a matter of theory, Uroum Bashou. Now that kittens are missing, it is vital that you make the books reveal what they know.'

'Missing kittens are never a good thing.'

'A cat must take note of that,' Tag suggested, 'where he might ignore other things.'

she reached the stairs to the ground floor the air was rank and solid, a substance rather than a smell. Leo hesitated, and lifted her head to listen. The mutter of conversation from the Library had grown faint and comfortless; three more steps down and it faded altogether. She was alone in a brown gloom, in some sort of stone-floored hallway. When she ran she could hear the shush and patter of her own paws. She stopped. She half-turned back. She listened. Something touched her foot. She stiffened. She leapt away. It was the head of a discarded broom, as big as a cat, its bristles chewed off by time. She crept back, neck extended, to make sure it was dead. Other objects loomed in the hall: a bag of cement, half-empty; some broken floorboards; a dusty bicycle wheel propped up against the wall. An old coat on a hook looked like a human being.

Eventually she came to the kitchen. There she wandered about for some minutes, nosing into corners, pushing her head into a chipped enamel breadbin to inhale its ghosts of mice, jumping up to teeter along the rim of the old sink. She skirted a pile of old leather shoes. Until she was satisfied it was unoccupied, she kept to the margins of the room. Then she trotted into the middle of it to have a look at the kitchen table, with its ancient chequered-plastic tablecloth. The rank odour was thick and solid there. Leo looked up and saw her mistake. 'Oh no,' she thought. The hair went up on her back. Staring away from the table as hard as she could, she began to inch out of the room. No decision of hers was involved. She directed her eyes down and away; and, very stiffly, and slowly, and carefully, her legs began to take her towards the door. Ever since she came into the kitchen, the guardian of that place had been sitting on the table-top in the soup of his own smell, watching her.

'And what are you?' he said quietly. 'What are you, I wonder?'

He was an enormous, dirty, half-maimed old marmalade tomcat, with a broad flat head and ears chewed to mere frills of flesh a dirty pink colour. One cheek had collapsed, bashed in perhaps by some hurrying car or angry human foot: snaggle-teeth protruded on that side and, viewed

'Nothing,' said Leonora.

The gatekeeper sat down and scratched himself again. 'His skin itches, but he welcomes that,' he mused. 'His ears grow deaf, but he welcomes that. Kater Murr is a cat in a million.' Waves of bad smell issued from him.

He studied Leo and concluded, 'Come to Kater Murr, my dear. You're enough to make anyone wonder.'

Leo turned her head away from him.

Somehow she had got herself against a wall.

'Come to the gatekeeper.'

'Empty speech, Kater Murr,' said a voice from the hallway behind him.

'Tag!' called Leonora.

At that exact moment there was a flurry of violence in the kitchen, a savage hiss, a scratch and shuffle of claws on tile. Paws were splayed, teeth were bared in the gloom, aggressive postures struck then suddenly folded. Light flickered off the points and edges of things. Everything seemed confused, too quick, too real, and Leo thought she was trapped in the kitchen with two much larger animals, one made of brass and the other of silver. It was only for an instant. Kater Murr's smell flooded sickeningly over everything – then another smell, of musk and winter, powder snow on an icy wind, washed it away. There was a distant, fading roar. Then the Majicou was standing amiably beside her and saying, 'I think we can go now, Leonora.'

She stared at him.

'Did you see that?' she said.

'See what?'

'In here. I— Never mind. You couldn't have seen anything from the hall.'

Tag shook himself to settle his fur.

'Not from out there,' he agreed.

In the yard, somewhat recovered, she asked him, 'So: what have we learned?'

Tag considered this gravely.

'I don't know about you,' he said; 'but I've learned that Uroum Bashou has a more unruly servant than I imagined.'

Leonora shivered.

After he had waited two hours for her, he had to admit she wasn't coming. By then, he had other problems.

Everyone else had vanished too.

He prowled the oceanarium, or sat outside on its doorstep. He searched the lanes and rooftops round about, calling, 'Cy! Rags! Pertelot!' but he didn't dare go far in case they arrived while he was gone.

'Leonora!' he called. 'You bad kitten!'

While he thought, 'It was wrong of me to tease her like that in the house of Uroum Bashou. I was just showing off.'

In the shadows by the oceanarium door, a spiral iron stairway led to the lip of the fish-tank. From there you could look down on the water, itself bathed in the greenish light of the powerful aquarium lamp. Tag climbed it and looked down on the little sharks, turning and weaving in the hallucinatory light and silent tranquillity. They reminded him of dogs, unassuagable and muscular dogs: though they had a quality of patience no land animal could ever possess.

He hated them.

but it was in Jackson Square her real targets lay – the hot-dog stands, the bars and the trash cans from which an enter-prising cat (a cat like herself) could con a meal for one; with luck, for two. This would mean crossing Decatur. Sealink and Red sat on the edge of the kerb and stared up and down. The four-lane street was busy with traffic: a bizarre mixture of modern automobiles and mule-drawn carts – gaily painted in bright pastel colours for the tourist trade – one of which hove into view.

'I'm Joey, and this here's my mule, Shine,' they heard the elderly carter explain to his passengers, a pair of thin Japanese youngsters clutching cameras and guidebooks; and a large couple in matching warm-up suits they had bought in Biloxi. 'Eats like a elephant and pulls like a ox, when she ain't standing still, which is what she most prefers. She knows I don't carry no whip, and sometimes she likes to take advantage.'

Shine stared patiently through her blinkers at the ground between her feet. Complicated harness-lines and traces looped across her back and a bright red human's hat was perched on top of her head. Someone had cut rough holes in the fabric, through which the mule's ears sprouted indig-nantly. A curious fellow feeling stole over the calico. Other animals she'd never had much time for – there were always so many cat-things to do – but something about the mule's trammelled patience took her attention.

'Hey, hon,' Sealink said softly, walking up under Shine's nose. 'Don't be so downcast. Sun's out and all. Least there's only five of them to haul.'

The mule turned its velvet muzzle to her, sniffed cautiously.

'*You* say that.'

'I do.'

A wicked light came into her dark eye. 'Do you know how I got my name?' she asked obliquely.

'No.'

'Jes' take care that you watch when I gets down the street a little ways.'

By now, the carter was in the driving seat and was well

Food. Of course; food. Spicy food. Boudin with chilli sauce . . .

McIlhenny's Tabasco.

Sauce of the devil.

Nothing like it in all the world. Its arsonous memory licked across her tongue, to sear dark thoughts away.

'You hungry, or something?'

The big marmalade was watching her with interest. Feeling his gaze upon her, Sealink shook herself out of her reverie.

'Why you starin' at me like that?'

'You're droolin'.'

'Then I guess it's time to eat.'

'Thank the Lord.'

The two cats snaked between human feet, slipped through the traffic on Decatur and headed down St Louis, past the French Market Inn towards the Napoleon House. At the junction with Chartres, a mule-cart was stationary by the side of the road. Joey the carter was sitting on the sidewalk with his head in his hands. Shine tossed her head gently from side to side to make her bit-rings jingle. She had no passengers left at all.

The two cats turned right and ran down the sidewalk, keeping close to the shadows, beneath balconies of curlicued ironwork and windows blinded by peeling shutters in the pastel colours of faded silk flowers; under cars and pick-ups, from one point of cover to the next.

Sealink strode out in front, trotting backwards to communicate her enthusiasm face to face. 'Babe: you're going to love this place, I swear. Finest damned shrimp this side of the Gulf, and I should know, 'cause I've been around the whole darn world and I've ate the best of the best. Hmm-mmm. Been eating here since you was a twinkle in your Momma's eye.'

'Sure don't look older than a twinkle yourself.'

'Why that's real poetic, hon,' Sealink told him. 'You-all make that up yourself?'

Red pretended to study something at the end of the street.

a marmalade with an odd eye, was staring nervously at them both.

'Hey!' said the chef. 'You can't come around here, baby.'

Sealink turned the purr up a notch, to a volume that would clean rust off a boiler.

'This gentleman and I go way, way back,' she told Red. 'Pecan-coated drumfish a specialty. Oh yes.'

So saying, she raised her head to give the bearded man the benefit of her most adoring gaze. That gaze promised volumes. It promised deep rewards for the right contender. From Ankara to Zeebrugge, that gaze had divorced humans from their cooking. It had not failed her yet.

Red looked on, somewhat at a loss.

'Now come on, honey,' the big man said, as she fawned around his ankles one more time. 'You tryin' to bring me trouble?'

Sealink, meanwhile, was giving Red the hard stare.

'So,' she said. 'You're my pimp, or something? Are you gonna *earn* your dinner? Or am I the only one to have to humiliate myself today?'

Red returned her gaze for a moment longer than was necessary for mere politeness, then abruptly looked away. Dipping his head, he started to bump it somewhat shame-facedly against the chef's trousers, purring as best he might.

The chef looked pained.

'Come on, Red,' he protested. 'Two against one ain't fair.'

Red was delighted.

'Hey, he knows my name!'

Sealink sighed.

'Look at yourself a moment, babe. Was he going to call you Blackie?'

The big man glanced warily up and down the street, and seemed to come to a decision.

'Hell, I can't have you starve. Though–' he regarded Sealink askance ' – it don't look like you're in much danger of that, to me.'

He disappeared inside and returned a moment later bearing a large dish of orangey-pink shells, which smelled

Their eyes were dull. None of them was looking at Sealink or Red: instead their attention was fixed with horrible avidity upon the dish of crawfish.

Red had got close to the bottom of the bowl and was doggedly chasing the remaining food around with his mouth. Impatience made him clumsy. Bits of shell were pushed over the edge, where they fell with a papery whisper to the ground. There, propelled by a breath of wind, one drifted past Sealink and was at once seized upon by three of the silent cats. Ignoring the calico completely, they ragged feebly backwards and forwards at the shell, snarling and hissing between locked teeth.

Red looked up, saw the newcomers and jumped backwards in horror. With a howl and a huge leap he hurled himself clear into the road and ran off.

'Thanks a bunch, hero,' Sealink muttered.

Rarely averse to a fight, the calico nevertheless considered with some anxiety the situation confronting her. She was to all intents and purposes alone, since the only thing that could now be seen of Red was the bob of an orange tail-tip disappearing around the corner of the Rue Conti, while all around her were twenty deranged-looking cats. Not the best of odds. She'd already had one scrap since arriving back in the city of her birth. It was becoming tedious.

They crept closer, drawn by the smell from the dish. Sealink's eyes glinted. They were in a tight bunch now, too compact a group to charge through, too many to leap over. Instead, she inserted a paw under the dish and flipped it skywards, where it spun and wobbled for a moment, showering down scraps as it went. As above, so below: beside themselves with panic and voracity, the ferals scattered in twenty different directions, fanning out across the ground in eerie mirror image of the flying crawfish. Flakes of shell and meat rained down upon the sidewalk. In the havoc that ensued, Sealink picked her moment and wove with statuesque grace through the squabbling, empty-eyed cats, out into the road.

For a moment, she looked back, puzzled, still hearing something in her head, still catching the faded echo of that on lookin' at me and lickin' his black ol' lips, and it ain't nice: would you go ask him to stop?"'

Sealink grinned, despite herself.

'I see,' she said, 'that you have et some of that particular catfish in your time.'

He acknowledged this to be true.

'So what's happened to your sad sorry-ass tale of a vagabond no self-respectin' female would want to be seen with?'

'Where's the self-respect in rolling on your back for any traveller comes along?' countered Red. He struck a pose. 'They were as cheap as trash. I had my way with them and said *bonsoir*. I ate them up because they did not capture my heart.'

Sealink narrowed her eyes and regarded him with interest. If times had changed since she was one of those little boardwalk queens herself, male attitudes sure hadn't.

'So, babe,' she said, allowing some of the honey-dripping South onto her tongue. 'Tell me a little about yourself, and these females got you into such trouble. 'Cause you sure got a way with you and I expect there is a number of tales to tell of their feckless behaviour and lack of moral inhibition . . .'

Warm and luxuriant as her coat, her voice could twine round a receptive tomcat like a sweet Louisiana vine. Had her considerable conquests agreed to pool their experience, many would have admitted to not listening attentively to the content of her conversation, bathed as they were in the lilt of those soft Southern vowels, lulled into what might well soon prove to be a false sense of security; for who knew how an independent calico cat with a powerful will and determined ways might deal with a dreamy tomcat off his guard?

Red's eyes had become vague and unfocused. He forgot, for a moment, what he had been about to say.

'Hey!' he said. 'I—'

He shook himself suddenly and looked around.

But Sealink had stalked on ahead, tail up and haunches swaying provocatively. Let the famous love 'em and leave 'em Lothario see what he was missing.

*

was a pedigree Maine Coon? Her and her husband, they took me in, put a diamanté collar round my neck and called me Minouche.'

Red snorted. 'Ain't people ridiculous?'

'They sure can be self-deceiving,' she agreed, 'in their vanity and greed.'

And this was the story she told him –

'They fed me, and I grew. It was tinned food, hon, and gourmet scraps. I musta gained a good five pounds.' Sealink smoothed the fur over her belly contemplatively. (Actually, she wasn't too sure she hadn't put that weight back on again . . .) 'But they deluded themselves about that the same as they'd deluded themselves about my ancestry. Plain truth is, I was carryin', hon. Their beautiful "pedigree Maine Coon" had been knocked up a week or so before by some mangy boardwalk tomcat just like you, babe. So it was with considerable horror that the female opened the linen closet one morning to discover that "Minouche" had spawned five tiny little Minouches, all over her best Egyptian cotton sheets.

'It was a messy business, hon, but surely no excuse for what followed—'

'I ain't listenin' to this,' said Red. But he was.

'They took those kittens offa me that same morning. For days I quartered the apartment, searching for my babies.'

On the fifth day, at the corner of the open bedroom door, she'd stopped stone-still, sure she'd heard a distant whimper. It ceased. She'd stood there for some time, her ears rotating and all her will bent on locating the sound. When she had started to search again, the heart-rending whimper returned, at the outer edges of her senses. Whatever she did, she could not place it. Some minutes later she'd realized that it was her own voice she was hearing, a constant, mechanical lament.

'The next day, they took me in a wicker cage to a building downtown.'

It stank of fear and pain and disinfectant. Inside were animals crouching in boxes and baskets. Those that could see out had turned to stare at her.

Twilight saw the two cats back at the deserted Moonwalk. They had, by a stroke of fantastic luck, stumbled upon some redfish heads in an alley yet to be discovered by the starving ferals, and choked down flesh and eyes and scales as if they might never eat again. Above them, the sky had darkened to ultramarine, and the air took on a sultry, tangible feel, as if someone had upturned a bowl over the city, trapping inside it all the oxygen everyone had breathed that day. All along the river's edge, the insects had come to life: a million tiny chainsaws whining and buzzing. Mosquitoes darted about the shoreline, seeking blood to suck. Dragonflies – hawks of the insect world – whirred after them, their neon glinting green and blue. All around, invisible to even a cat's eye, the crickets set up their nightly chirring.

Shamed by the calico's tale of sorrow into a confessionary frame of mind, Red had started to tell Sealink something of his own life.

'I'm not proud of some of the things I done. Treated a few ladies badly in my time; but, hell, I been treated bad enough myself. Fell for a little queen down near the Square a couple of years back. Téophine, she was called. Thought that was a real pretty name at the time. She was all black and white and neat – made me feel like a lumberin' fool. She was always ready for a chase. She'd nip me and run off, pretend to be alarmed when I followed, then when I caught up, all out of breath, she'd throw herself down on the ground at my feet, roll on her back and twist all around. Then as soon as I got up the nerve to approach her, she'd be all teeth and claws and a flash of white feet. Next thing I knew, she'd be up on a fence laughing down at me. Never knew where I was with her. I guess I was just kinda naïve, didn't realize what it was she wanted from me. Wouldn't make the same mistake now . . .

'Two days later she's rolling around under the bushes in the park with some old stripy tomcat with frills instead of ears. Thought my heart would stop right there and then. She wouldn't even look at me after that.

'From then on, I guess I didn't care much for anyone. Scattered my favours around. Made a few of those little foot might end up if left unattended.

Sealink grinned. 'Hey, Baron! Baron Raticide!'

The old cat's head wobbled for a moment as if registering some distant sound. Then he swayed on, borne along by his own weird internal rhythms.

Sealink ran to catch up with him. She bounded in front of him, pushed her face into his. His cataract-filled eyes flickered with life at her scent for a second, then he shuffled around her and continued his walk, still muttering.

'Come on, Baron, it's me!'

'Another of your "friends"?' Red asked the calico sardonically, keeping pace with the old cat.

Ignoring the marmalade, Sealink ran suddenly ahead up the boardwalk and started to – Red could think of no other word for it – dance. She lifted first one front paw, then the other, then her hind feet in the same way; then she started to spin like a kitten trying to catch its tail, all the time howling:

> 'In the heat of the night
> When the time is right
> And the moon hangs over the river
> Queens make their cry
> And blood runs high
> Hearts start to quiver and shiver . . .'

The Baron lumbered over to the dancing calico. Suddenly he was matching her step for step, and as he danced so his movements became fluid and powerful, age and madness lost in another form of lunacy altogether. At last the two cats were whirling together, the Baron's black shape a shadow to the harlequin patterns of Sealink's leaping form. Red felt his own feet start to move of their own accord, as the familiar rhythms crawled under his skin, and he began to make his own dance down amongst the boulders on the strand. Meanwhile, Baron Raticide's cracked old voice rose to join with the calico's wail for the final verse:

And he was off again, the dull light back in his eye, the sway back in his step. Sealink watched him shamble off into the night: Baron Raticide, a big black cat once lord of the boardwalk, high priest of the midsummer ritual, a proud, valiant tom who had ruled his roost and fathered kittens on every fertile queen from Algiers to the Armstrong Park; now reduced to a mad old vagrant. Looking at his retreating figure, hope withered anew and Sealink felt as if all the world had grown old and tarnished.

A light breeze was starting to raise peaks and troughs on the oily surface of the river. Red shivered. Despite the red-snapper heads and the crawfish it had been an odd sort of day. Instead of finding Téophine, he'd been bitten by an antsy calico cat and had danced with an old tramp. What was the world coming to?

Little swirls of dust and bits of rubbish started to blow around the boardwalk. A yellowing piece of newspaper fluttered past and lodged itself against the legs of the nearest bench. Red didn't even feel like chasing it.

'Come on, babe,' he called softly to the distracted calico. 'Let's go find that old Creole Queen, see what she can tell us.'

He wandered over and nudged Sealink out of her grim stupor. She blinked once or twice, then turned and butted her forehead against his cheek. Surprised at this sudden rough affection, Red took a step back. 'You don't have to knock me out, you know.'

'Seems you just ain't up to my weight, honey.'

Dodging in and out of the streetlights on the Moonwalk, the two cats disappeared into the night.

The yellowing sheet of paper that Red had dismissed as a page from an old *Times Picayune* was something far more relevant, and more sinister than he could have guessed.

It was a city ordinance.

Framed in formal language, it was addressed to the human inhabitants of New Orleans:

PART TWO

Messages From the Dead

VII

The Wisdom of Fishes

Tag sat alone in the oceanarium.

Outside it was deep night, the sea under cloud, the rooftops of the village tumbling away downhill in shadowed disorder. Inside, the light fell across the side of his face: the fishes slipped and turned, or hung motionless surrounded by tiny glittering motes.

'I don't know what to do,' he thought.

He had looked for Cy in all her favourite places. Nothing. The Beach-O-Mat was closed. The amusement arcades were closed. The docks were deserted, the fishing-boats at sea. Rag-mop palms shook themselves uneasily in the onshore wind in the moonless dark, and the fish-and-chip papers that blew up and down the sea front were empty and cold. He had combed the steep lanes between the cottages on Mount Syon and Tinnery, to find only empty doorsteps and household cats who made off hastily when they realized who he was. In the end, driven by anxieties he could barely express, he had taken the wild road to the windy spaces of Tintagel, where he found himself patrolling the headland crying, 'Ragnar! Pertelot!' until his voice cracked. Nothing. Nothing but the wild gorse, the empty church.

Cy had vanished.

The King and Queen were nowhere to be found.

Worst of all, Leo was still out there somewhere on the Old Changing Way, lost, puzzled, in need of help.

He remembered how, in the days of his own apprenticeship, he had run off by himself and got lost. 'That's the trouble with being the Majicou,' he thought. 'Your trainee is always going missing.'

Even as he was thinking, something happened to the light

He crept forward cautiously and sniffed his friends. Suddenly they seemed strange to him. A curious, baked warmth clung to them, as if they had brought back not just the smells but the climate of another country. They were rich with adventures he had not shared.

'Hush,' they reassured him. 'Tag, we're the same cats you knew. But listen.'

And this was what they told him –

That evening, while Tag and Leonora were still travelling the wild roads, the King and the Queen had eaten a fish supper with Cy outside the amusement arcade. Afterwards, the three of them had strolled along the sea front in the dark so Pertelot could stare at the lights of the fishing-boats on the edge of the bay and whisper, 'Oh Rags, what a perfect night!' To please the tabby, the Queen had even put her perfect nose round the door of the Beach-O-Mat (though to Cy's disappointment she could not be persuaded to go in and watch the human washing spin round). Back at the oceanarium she and the King had slept soundly, only to be woken by a disturbance. The light had changed. There were noises above. Behind the glass, shoals of frightened mackerel waved goodbye like a thousand human fingers.

'It was as if something had broken the surface of the water in the tank,' Pertelot Fitzwilliam told Tag. 'My first thought was that something had arrived there. That was how I put it to myself, Mercury: that something had arrived there.' She shivered. 'I always hated that water.'

'Her second thought,' said Ragnar, 'was of Cy.' He paused for effect. 'I am afraid to say, my friend, that she was gone.'

'I woke Rags. Together we searched the building.' The Queen looked around ironically. 'It didn't take long. Cy was nowhere to be found. Had she fallen in the tank? We had to know!'

Step by step, their bodies elongated by caution, each paw placed in a furious silence, they had crept up the spiral stairs to look down into the water in its blaze of electric light –

Nothing.

'Whatever that is,' said Cy. 'He tells me stuff about that but I just don't pay attention. Listen, it's lucky I fell in, because today this fish comes with a message for you. Around and about in the ocean by Tintagel Head he's met some guys. They aren't fish, he says. They don't breathe water. They shouldn't even *be* down there! But he's been told to fetch you and take you to some old place he knows. Maybe you'll find Odin and Isis there, Ray's not clear on that. Anyway, you got to go with him.'

She lowered her voice.

'*Under the water*,' she said.

'Never,' said Pertelot. 'Let me up!'

But, even as she spoke, the great fish began to sink. His passengers were submerged instantly.

'Ragnar Gustaffson!' called the Queen, darting this way and that in panic. 'How dare you let this happen!' There was no escape. All she could do was stand and tremble. 'Rags,' she whispered in despair. 'Oh Rags.' But Ragnar stood as straight and tall as he could beside her, and that reminded her who she was: and they soon found to their astonishment that they were still dry. They could breathe. They were beneath the water but somehow not in it. The oceanarium was already gone, replaced by a huge, dim, ribbed architecture. They were in something like an infinite gloomy hallway under the sea. Endless lugubrious echoes rolled away down it. Shoals of tiny fish-souls ran everywhere, like two-dimensional silver streams. Vast shadowy forms boomed and groaned past, fish so large they made Ray seem like a mote settling in a glass of water.

Ragnar laughed suddenly.

'This is what I *call* an adventure,' he said.

'I can't believe this,' said Pertelot. 'I'm dreaming this.'

'See?' said Cy excitedly. 'What I'm trying to say: fishes have their secrets in this wide world too! They got things we don't know about, such as that tank is an entrance to some long-ago Fish Road of their choice!'

Those roads are as difficult as any. They are travelled on a notion, an idea inside. For what seemed like hours, the ray manoeuvred and sideslipped through the enormous space as yawning in its stern – he was barely more than a boy – wore the turban of a barge-captain, to which he seemed entitled only by ambition. He was half-asleep when the ray called Ray, monstrous with journeys and still moving at the speed of the Fish Road, erupted from the water off his starboard bow, cut a steep, whistling, iridescent arc north to south against the sky, and plunged back into the river again. The felucca rocked and staggered. Displaced water raced outwards in huge ripples which, rebounding elastically from bank to bank, churned the surface of the river into spray. Egrets burst up from the reeds; doves panicked into the sky from the whitewashed dove-castle in the village, their wings clapping urgently. The young man leapt to his feet and clung to the mast of his boat for support, rubbing his eyes in astonishment. Perched like a pilot on the back of the giant fish, just behind its strange flat head, he had glimpsed a small tabby cat with white bib and paws.

More cats, turning over and over, fell out of the air into the roiling water a few yards distant. This was too much for him. He shrugged.

'It can only be the will of God,' he said.

Green water closed over the Mau and she sank, all bubbles and frantic legs, and the splendour and mystery of her ride on the great fish evaporated to nothing. Water is water, wherever you try to breathe it. The Nile was warmer than the canal at Piper's Quay, but no easier to negotiate with. Soon, she couldn't even remember when she was drowning, then or now. There was a high, singing noise inside her head. 'Oh Rags,' she thought. 'I do hate this. And I can't even see you.' Once, she thought she could feel him near, locked in his own lonely struggle, and she tried to move towards him. Then that feeling was gone, and anyway there was nothing much left of Pertelot Fitzwilliam to feel it. For a while she was just a grim argument, carried on in the clutch of the Nile (whose meaning, partially glimpsed in her dreams of Egypt, she now saw clear and stark: the gift of water is not security but constant transformation, not rest but movement, not victory over the desert but fecundity in impressed by the taste of this Nile,' he told anyone who would listen as he thugged his way over the stern of the felucca. 'It is some rank stuff, as Tag would say.' He shook himself like a dog, squinted up into the sunlight, and, discovering his beloved Mau in the grip of Nagib the boatman, nipped forward smartly and bit the boy in the ankle. At exactly the same moment, the felucca, accelerating in the current and unguided except by God, ran heavily into the east bank. Nagib fell over. Pertelot cried, 'Ragnar Gustaffson, don't you dare let anything like this happen to me again!' Tearing out further gravel and mud, which fell softly into the Nile like wet brown sugar in a saucer of tea, the boat ground along the bank.

As soon as it came to rest, the two cats jumped nimbly ashore.

They fled through the palm and lemon groves, where insects were already droning in pools of hot greenish light, along the beaten paths, up towards the village, which, partly shadowed by the dark terraces above it, still lay asleep. Cool air moved in the narrow crooked lanes between the houses, whose lower walls remained in a lavender shade even as the sun struck like running gold across their roofs. Goats chewed thoughtfully in a rising side street, where the earth was cracked and dry and strewn with dung: Pertelot hurried, apparently unremarked, between their delicate hooves, while Ragnar begged her to slow down and think. 'There's no need to run now!' But, when she stopped, she only caught the smell of the human being on her coat and panicked again. Towards the edge of the village, the desert wind blew feathery skeins of sand across the lanes. Suddenly, the damp river airs had evaporated, the ground rose steeply away from the houses. It was the end of vegetation. Terrace succeeded stony terrace. Entering the ancient quarries of the tomb-builders, Pertelot began to call, 'Isis! Odin!' She disappeared suddenly against heaps of spoil the exact colour of her coat. 'Wait!' called Rags when he next saw her, rose-grey against the shadows. She looked back at him for a second, her tail agitated with nerves or bodies glowing softly off the cold stone in ochres and terra-cotta reds, Nile earths, desert earths, the black and white details as sharp as the day they were painted. They were, the Mau thought, just what you would expect from human beings. Animal-headed gods whose expressions, sidelong and uneasy despite their arrogance, soon revealed them to be men in masks. Gods who feared other gods. Gods who gathered meaningless objects to them. Gods desperate for life yet so clearly in love with death. Their postures were stiff with denial: but, however they had tried to halt it, time had parted around them and rushed on.

Out of their failure, with a secret smile and kohl-blackened eyes full of delight in the world, danced a single goddess. She wore sandals, a white tunic, necklaces of garnet and lapis lazuli. Her limbs were sensual and long, her name as forgotten as the pictographic language of the Missing Dynasty itself. In the pictures she was often shown accompanying some long-buried king, her slim hand upon his shoulder, his arm about her waist. She had gathered her followers to her: musicians and dancers and celebrants; and, all around her delicate feet, cats! The cats were dancing too, or so it seemed. Suddenly, in the next picture, the goddess was a cat, too! Huge and tawny, her eyes the deep, fecund green of the desert oases, she danced among them. They were lithe and ancient-looking. They were purring and rubbing their sleek heads against her ankles, or against each other. And two of them were depicted separately, in a sequence of cartouches, which, the Mau was quick to see, told a story –

She sat down.

She thought, 'Well!'

The cats seemed almost to move before her eyes. She was soon so caught up in their lives she forgot her own.

A minute passed, and then another. After a third, the light in the tomb was faintly disturbed, and there was a sound like a single drop of water falling into a pool.

The cats on the wall were a male and a female, with all the simplicity and grace of the goddess herself. She was shown smiling down on them with a special favour, while but not perhaps as dangerous as the thing in the corner of the tomb.

'Pertelot!' Rags cried.

She was creeping towards it on her belly, her eyes quite blank and empty, while it bowed and wobbled over her like a spinning-top about to fall: a dense eccentric whirligig of human debris – the black loess of ancient organs, bits of bone, flakes of bandage and parchment – a dust-storm of mummia and old death six or seven feet broad at its top, balanced on a tiny shifting base and reaching from floor to ceiling. It was aware. It seemed to be arguing with itself. From it issued bad smells, intermittent, disconnected voices, blasts of hot and cold air, and a strange, thready music. As the Mau got closer, it sensed her presence. A shudder passed through it. Lights flickered deep inside. Suddenly it bellied towards her like smoke in the wind, breaking up into dusty smuts and cinders. There was a deep groan. Then chanting began. Someone was chanting in there. At this, Pertelot went rigid. All along her spine the fur was up on end. Stiff-legged, a pace at a time, she moved towards it. She hated the vortex but it was like a magnet to her. In response it pulsed and roared and shot up to the ceiling –

'I think we have had enough of this,' announced the King of Cats.

He sprang forward, got a good grip of his wife's tail with his mouth, and yanked her backwards. Pertelot yowled and spat. He closed his eyes, and, offering up a silent apology, pulled harder. It was a grim struggle. Ragnar splayed his cobby legs and backed away, losing most of every inch he gained. Pertelot, her signals as crossed, fought both sides at once with a dour, indiscriminate passion. The whole world stank of cinders. The whirlwind staggered and wobbled over the two of them like a drunk with raised hands. 'We're for it now!' thought Ragnar. But even as it fell upon them it was breaking up. There was a faint 'pop!' a puff of foul wind. Dust pattered on the floor of the tomb like a sudden shower of rain.

Ragnar sat down heavily as Pertelot stopped pulling away from him. The Mau shook herself; looked round puzzledly back to Tintagel. Look! Here they are in the king's chamber, Discerning Invisible Things. Afterwards, imprinted in the bright tapestry of their eyes the king sees and is able to identify the ghosts that disturb his sleep. He can have peace at last! In return, he grants the cats – and their kittens, and their kittens' kittens in perpetuity – the freedom of the land.'

'They are us,' Ragnar insisted. 'We are them.'

'Oh Rags,' she said.

'They are doing that quite well,' he went on with satisfaction, after he had had another look at the picture which showed the ancestors mating. 'But not as well as us.'

'Rags!'

'He is not as black as me.'

She laughed.

'His fur is not so long.'

'You child,' she said.

A cold wind curled round them suddenly, lifting the dust into their eyes. Electricity unzipped the air, filled it with the taste of metal. There were stealthy sounds. A cough. A rising hum, as of a child's top. They jumped to their feet, fur on end. Rubbish was being drawn up from all over the tomb, whirled about, sucked into a corner.

'Run!' called Ragnar.

Too late. The whirlwind had assembled itself again. Pace by pace, shaking with delirium, her eyes lit up from within like lamps, Pertelot was tugged towards it. For a moment its rotation seemed slow. It wobbled. Toppled. Turned a startling Nile green, then back to black. There was music from within – bells, a reed flute, small drums arrhythmic and perverse. There were movements, as of a dance or struggle. A figure, perhaps human, became dimly visible within the swirling rubbish and mummia dust. It was as simple as the painted figures on the wall. It leaned forward. It spoke.

'I have two of your kittens,' it said. 'Give me the third and I will spare your lives.' Suddenly a second figure seemed to curdle out of the dust. It dragged the first one, struggling, out of sight. A friendlier voice said, 'The Golden Cat is not what it seems.'

Rags darted forward.

where pieces of sculpture a hundred feet high had begun to lean against one another like very old men. The whirlwind raged and howled. It grew.

'Hurry!'

Stark shapes of darkness and light. Squinting into the gale, Rags and Pertelot teetered on the edge of a steep black ramp above a drop they could not measure. Dust boiled up and streamed off into the vortex behind them.

'This way! Into the wind!'

They flitted across a pillared ante-room and out into the forecourt of the temple. The light was so strong they could feel it scrape the surface of their eyes. Midday. The stone sang with it. The Nile below was lost in heat-shimmer. Down through the quarries they fled, to the edge of the village, where the goats, rooting senselessly among stones, sought shade at the base of the houses. Here, where heat had emptied the lanes and even the dove-castle seemed empty, Ragnar halted suddenly.

'Look!' he said.

'Rags, come on!'

'It isn't following us any more,' he said. 'Look!'

Through the heat haze, the tomb entrances could be seen like low black slots against the yellowish, crumbling slopes of the hills above. From each of them there now issued a thick, slow, sulphurous gout of dust. A low rumble reached the ears of the cats. The earth shook, as if something had settled. The dust clouds rose lazily into the hot air, a dozen coiling roseate smudges against a sky like heated brass. There was a long pause, in which Pertelot and Ragnar eyed one another uneasily. Then, with a renewed rumbling and shaking of the earth, as of gigantic forces in conflict, dust began to rise again – this time from the hills themselves. The tombs and temples of the Missing Dynasty were falling in one by one, taking an entire range of hills with them like collapsing paper bags.

'After that,' the Queen told Tag in the oceanarium, 'it was like a long dream.'

They had made their way down through the lemon groves

'Finally we reached the sea.'

The boat lay all morning not far outside the Eastern Harbour bar at Alexandria, its sail tightly furled in the dead-still air. Behind it, against a sky darkened with clouds, the fifteenth-century fortress of Qa'it Bey stood on its low headland like an illuminated model, yellow walls soaking up the hot and stormy light. That morning, before making the inexplicable decision to take two cats out to sea and wait there for whatever happened to him, its captain had put on a freshly-laundered white djellaba. It was his birthday. He was exactly thirty-five years old when the biggest ray he had ever seen surfaced from the Mediterranean fifty yards to seaward and began to make its way towards him. It was too late to flee. Besides, perched on the back of the fish, its fur steaming in the hot sun, was a small tabby cat. Within minutes the other two cats had leapt delicately off the bow of the felucca and joined her there; the great fish had submerged; the sea was flat and calm again.

The captain rubbed his eyes.

'*In scha'Allah*,' he said, and turned towards the shore.

contrast to the shambles of flesh which comprised her great body, Kiki's limbs, protruding stiffly beneath her as if they had simply collapsed there and then under her weight, were stick-thin, her tail hairless as a nutrea rat's.

Sealink shivered with sudden, instinctive repulsion.

Red hung back, uncertain.

As the calico moved into her line of sight, the yellow queen blinked faster. She squinted, blinked again. A tiny flame of recognition sparked in the depths of those cold amber eyes. Then she yawned, displaying teeth orange with decay, a white-coated tongue.

A strange listlessness now overcame the courtiers. Their dullness sharpened into anticipation. As one they swivelled to regard the newcomer.

'*Eh bien*, it is the Delta Queen. I'd heard you were back. It's been a while, *cher*. You've gotten *plus grosse*.'

Sealink felt the fur on the back of her neck rearrange itself.

'I could say the same, and more.'

The yellow queen laughed – the sound of a hacksaw on damp wood. 'Time has treated me better than you, *cher*. You look – how can I put this without making *le faux pas*? A little worn, perhaps: a little longer of tooth and claw, ha? Maybe learned a lesson or two and come back to your hometown sadder and wiser and in need of some help from La Mère?'

'I'm here to find my kittens.'

A wave of reaction seemed to pass through the yellow queen and on through her courtiers. It was nothing so definite as surprise; rather an acknowledgement, a shared understanding, but there was no warmth in the response. Kiki La Doucette straightened, heaved herself upright. She smiled, so that an evil orange slit opened beneath her wide pink muzzle.

'Oho, we all want the *kittens*, *cher*.'

Sealink stared at her.

'Do you know where they are?' she persisted.

Kiki's eyes glittered.

'Kittens are like stones on the beach, *cher*. How should I know which are your brood?'

an intimidating proposition; but this female was a monster! The courtiers parted before him like a sea.

'I think I seen you before, ha? Ah yes, I remember you well. Kiki La Doucette is renowned for her remarkable memory. I know every cat on my boardwalk better than their own mothers. Hell, I am La Mère – I *am* the mother of most of those cats! Not you, though, *mon ange*, not with that ugly visage, that black stain like the devil's mark! *These* are my babies – '

She spread a paw wide to indicate her courtiers. A curiously rapacious tenderness informed her features as she surveyed this motley crew. Red followed her gaze. All different sizes they were, with fur of every colour and type that the Great Cat had created. Something was wrong, though. He couldn't quite hold the thought in his head, but he felt it deep inside. Something was lost here. Something was odd. A mangled tomcat returned Red's stare, then split lazily from the pack.

'What you lookin' at, boy?'

'You're wearing a collar.'

'It's an honour you gotta earn.'

'Where I come from, it's thought kinda demeaning. Only housecats wear collars; no self-respectin' feral would dream of it.'

'Well, boy, you can dream on, 'cause you ain't one of the Queen's own, and without you ain't one of us, you don't got no collar and no food neither. Hell, boy, you don't got no *life*!'

All around, the courtiers wheezed and spluttered with laughter, eyes screwed up in derision. The tom strutted back to the group, bony rump swaying.

'*Ferme ta gueule!*' The laughter withered to silence. 'So,' she addressed herself to Sealink again. 'You do one little thing for me, and I'll tell you something you'll like. A bargain, ha?'

'What is it?'

'You go down to the Golden Scarab, *cher*, and there you find two young ladies who call theyselves Venus and Sappho – ' a distant wheeze from the retinue ' – yeah, they them and make up for leaving them to the mercy of this town, I aim to do it.'

Red's mouth opened, then a thought slid into the patched eye and he promptly shut it again. At that moment another human being appeared, turning the corner by the bar at the end of the street and proceeding towards the Golden Scarab; a tall, gawky man in an ill-fitting linen jacket with creases that looked too random and ingrained to be deliberately casual. Without a glance at the two cats, he pushed at the bookshop door. It strained open on its stiff hinges, and at once the calico was inside, between his feet and straight under a dusty shelf. When Sealink stared back out, she could see Red faintly through the grime on the door, pressing his nose to the pane. His breath flowered and died on the glass.

The humans shuffled out to the back of the shop and disappeared. Sealink glanced cautiously around, then emerged from her hiding-place. She sniffed the air. Cats! At least two distinct scents, and another smell, too, that she could not quite place. Just as she was digesting this information, she caught sight of a plumed tail, switching away high above her. Backing off for a better view, she stared upwards. On the top shelf, stationed between two book-ends in the form of Anubis the jackal-headed god, was a large-furred tabby whose golden eyes shone brightly in the dingy interior. She had been dozing, but now all her attention was fixed on Sealink.

Calico and tabby stared at one another. The tabby bristled. Sealink felt her fur stand on end. Maintaining intense eye contact while staring upwards was something of a strain, Sealink found. After a while, she realized that she could feel the blood draining from her head, leaving it light and empty. Narrowing her eyes, she tried to focus on the cat above her. Black specks began to float in her vision. She felt hot, then cold. The world started to spin. Shadows twisted then fell apart; and all at once her nose was assailed with a complex and familiar scent: civet and attar of roses! Burnt spices! When she stared again into the gloom of the top shelf, the russet tabby had gone. Sitting in its place between

A laugh from all three men, then the sound of something heavy being dragged across the floor. A door opened and the voices retreated, dull, self-satisfied, full of the smugness of conspiracy.

'. . . to the Elysian Fields . . .'

'. . . for the Alchemist . . .'

'. . . Faubourg Marigny . . . kittens . . .'

Out of this empty mutter, Sealink's brain picked first 'Alchemist' and then 'kittens'. The world lurched. She stared at the tapestry curtain and a shudder passed through her great frame. What to depend upon among so many dreams and omens, so many uncertain signs? Lost kittens, old friends, past and future intermingled in these Crescent City blues of hers.

'Hey! You deaf or something?'

She jumped. Another cat had joined the tabby. It was equally large and well-furred and brindled all over with patches of orange and black, like some randomly marked tigress. The two were clearly sisters.

'So, I ask you again, you have come for La Mère's *petit cadeau* – you come to collect her gift, eh, *cher*?'

The newcomer's tone was hard but cultivated. Were they both daughters of Kiki La Doucette? Their father must have been some vast tomcat, Sealink thought, to have produced two such strapping offspring from a female who had once been as skinny as the high queen of the boardwalk.

Sealink looked the brindled cat up and down. Like the tabby, she wore a collar. Little charms and bells hung from it so that each motion produced a faint jingling. Housecats, she thought, derisively. Nothing more than pampered pets.

'Ain't no call to *cher* me, honey. I ain't running errands out of politeness.'

The brindled cat blinked superciliously at her. The tabby sniffed. 'There's no call for rudeness, either, especially from some renegade.'

'Who you calling renegade?' Sealink's tone was dangerous.

'*Cher*, you don't have no owner, you don't have no protector. You wear no collar, you not one of the saved.

139

stood up on her hind legs and examined the lid. Of all the objects in the storeroom, its surface alone was free of dust. Light falling from some obscure source had formed a golden pattern upon it, a tall triangle with a round head, somewhat like an old-fashioned keyhole, or the sun rising over a pyramid.

Sappho elbowed past her and started to lever at the heavy lid. The pattern of light dispersed into the general gloom. 'Lend a paw, Venus,' she hissed.

The second tabby looked startled and immediately leapt to her sister's aid. After some puffing and genteel swearing, the lid fell back with a creak and sat upright in the air, supported by two heavy leather hinges. Two furry rumps heaved at something within the chest, then emerged backwards, dragging some amorphous package with their teeth. Out in the uncertain light of the storeroom it looked like a badly-wrapped package – layers of creased brown paper coming away in flakes, girded around with lengths of chewed string. Sealink nosed at it. The object emitted a strange smell, rather like old carpet. Overlying this fustiness was a dense perfume which made her cough and sneeze. It was heavy and felt hard to the touch.

'Take this to La Mère. And be very careful with it.'

The two sisters exchanged a glance, the dull light flicking off their golden eyes. They turned to stare at the calico, their expressions identically opaque.

'If you meddle with it you will be sorry.'

'La Mère will make it so.'

Sealink met their stare unblinking.

'She don't scare me. This is just a job of work; means to an end.'

She bent her head to the knot of string. The problem with manoeuvring the object was not just its weight, but its awkward size. There was no dignified way to proceed. Following the two sisters to the rear door of the storeroom, Sealink put her back into the task, dragging the parcel until her teeth ached.

'Let's open it.'

'*Cher*, you performed a task for me and now I owe you a little bit of truth; but sometimes truth can be a painful thing. Maybe you not want to know what I know.'

Sealink sensed a double-cross. 'And why would that be?'

The yellow queen rearranged her vast bulk, as if settling into some long tale. 'Not all litters care to acknowledge their *maman*. Believe me, kittens can be mighty ungrateful, *cher*, their hearts as bitter as wormwood.' She wiped what appeared to be a completely dry eye with her paw. 'It can be most hurtful, when your very own kittens will not show you the love and respect you deserve. *Soixante jours*. Sixty days you carry them inside you. Sixty days of discomfort and anguish. You feed them; you give and give and give – oh, they suck so hard, it make you sore!'

She screwed her eyes tight shut and when she opened them again she had somehow contrived to make them shine with tears. Sealink looked on, unmoved and impatient.

'Cut the crap. Where can I find them?'

'Be polite!' the old queen admonished. 'You want them, you hear me out.' Her eyes flashed dangerously. 'And sometimes those who call you mother are not your own; and these are often the most grateful of all.

'You had five babies, *hein*? They were taken away very young. Taken and cast aside. The humans who had taken you into their home left your babies *avec le docteur*, to be disposed of in, as they say "a humane fashion"; but the vet's *assistant*, he is a greedy man. He save the money on the drugs that give them peaceful sleep: he leave them, just a few days old, out on the levee, wait for the tide to take them. That's where I found them. Two were almost dead, gasping out their last breaths. I watched, watched them die. Yes: I was their last sight, *les pauvres bébés*. For the other three, I was their mother, *cher: pas toi*. Three babies, and all so fine they became. Fine and big like the mother who ran away.'

A thought started to form in Sealink's head. It was unbearable. Kittens. When she thought of her kittens, it was as tiny scraps of fur: little balls of fluff no bigger than her paws, the way she had last seen them. Not as great big hollow beneath the boardwalk, dozing peaceably. When she opened her eyes just a slit, so that the world was comfortably blurred, she could see the moonlight on the Mississippi, a silver sheen like a secret wild road across the river. Kittens. What need did a cat of her age have of kittens? Let alone vast, snooty, tabby ones? Her trek from the Old World to the New had been no more than a wild-goose chase: a flurry of fuss and feathers. Well, she was still Sealink, and she would come to terms with this new disappointment. She shifted position, tucking her nose under her tail for added warmth, and was just starting to drift weightless among the stars when she became aware of another cat. Before she had time to register the scent, it had joined her in the hollow.

'Hey, gorgeous,' it said, its face obscured by the dark. 'Move over, make room for a cold and lonely boy.'

The calico grinned into the night.

Red felt her grin like the tiniest change in air pressure against his whiskers and rolled against her back. And in that position they fell asleep, head on each other's haunch, two cats alone against the world.

After that, the little tarmac road gave way to a lane heavily shaded by trees. The lane wasn't so neat. There was a narrow verge of vetches and couch grass; dog rose and nightshade, threaded through with old man's beard, made tangled screens through which the glitter of water could sometimes be seen where it ran shallow and clear in the sandy bottom of a ditch. Insects launched themselves clumsily out of the flowers and blundered past, scattering pollen from their feet and wings. The thick, drugged scent of meadowsweet came and went. 'I like this,' thought Animal X. A minute or two later, he remembered Stilton and the kitten. He turned round and found they were walking a few yards behind him. Stilton looked frail and tired already, but he was talking excitedly to the kitten. The kitten seemed puzzled. It was less distraught, though; and there seemed to be less anger in its silence. When he listened, Animal X could hear Stilton say, 'What you can get, you see, from the factory shop – '

They walked like this for some time. New sights waited round every corner. They saw human beings off in the distance across the fields. They saw a lake, green water that looked solid enough to stand on, with lily-pads and a heron on a post. They saw how the heat shimmered and danced above the land in the middle distance.

Towards midday the lane led them up to a broad black road down which huge energetic shapes roared and rushed. Waste paper blew up into the air, settled, blew up again. It was a very human place. There was a smell. Animal X and Stilton stood for a minute or two at the junction, wrinkling their noses, rocked dangerously by the passing airstream. Then they averted their faces in embarrassment – because they had forgotten, if they had ever known, what all this meant – and turned away. The kitten confronted things more stoically, as if it was determined to understand only the worst about the human world. It blinked its single eye.

Lupins filled the garden like candles. There was a scent of roses; of lavender. Everything was drowsy with summer air: the pony dreamed in its paddock, the dogs in their kennels dozed, the human beings murmured contentedly from their kitchens. The golden kitten stared into the twilight after the vanished ducks with a kind of absent-minded irritability, then followed Animal X and Stilton back up the hill, every so often shaking its head. Eventually they stood, the three of them, in front of a small weatherboard outhouse. White paint blistered, tarred roof entangled in honeysuckle, less a home improvement than an afterthought, this construction leaned amiably up against one of the cottages. From its partly open door – like beckoning human fingers, like tendrils of weed waving in deep water – issued smells both inviting and dangerous. Stilton raised his nose in the air. He drooled a little.

'Who's going first?' he said.

'We should think before we do anything,' said Animal X. Stilton sat down.

'I'm afraid anyway,' he said.

The kitten shouldered past them both.

'Wait,' recommended Animal X. 'We—'

Too late.

There was a scuffling sound inside, followed almost immediately by an outbreak of fierce yowling from the kitten. Behind that could be heard a deeper, more guttural complaint – the angry speech of some large unidentified animal. Stilton ran away down the garden. Animal X ran after him. When they stopped to look back, Stilton was still ahead but not by very much. Animal X felt ashamed of himself.

'We shouldn't let the kitten face whatever's in there on his own,' he said.

'No,' agreed Stilton.

'At least one of us should help.'

'You,' said Stilton. 'You go.'

The noise continued unabated, then rose to a crescendo. Animal X had crept halfway back down the garden path, and was crouching in a border of overgrown mint, when the sheer relief, pushed his face into the nearest of the bowls, and began eating. He had no idea what the stuff was, but his mouth didn't care. After a moment or two he became aware of the kitten standing next to him. He moved over.

'I don't know what cats eat when they're out on their own,' he said. 'But we can eat this. Go on, try some.'

The kitten tried. It ate slowly, and then faster. It raised its head and purred suddenly.

'You've got it all over your mouth,' said Animal X.

A little later, they both made room for Stilton.

'I like this,' Stilton said. 'It's almost as good as—'

'Shut up, Stilton.'

Outside, the dog – if indeed it was a dog, or had ever been one – stood completely still in the middle of the village. It was as large and as shapeless as it had ever been. It stood there, and it was the Dog. Its shapeless smell filled the summer air, overpowering for a moment the odours of honeysuckle and night-scented stock; and, to anyone walking past, its outline would have seemed to waver a little in the dusk.

It was thinking, 'I was comfortable in there.'

After a moment it thought, 'I would have eaten that stuff in the bowls.' It thought, 'Now those cats will eat it instead.' Finally it thought, 'The New Majicou – who is not the Old Majicou – asked for news of two golden kittens. There is one in that outhouse now. I know that. But one golden kitten is not two.' The dog mulled this over. 'There is no reward,' it concluded, 'for one golden kitten.'

But it decided to sleep the night quite near, so that it could follow them in the morning.

'A dog follows,' it thought comfortably.

It thought, 'That's what a dog does.'

The outhouse was filled with a curious rhythmic clanking sound. Every shred of food was gone: undeterred, the golden kitten had continued licking one of the empty metal dishes until it fetched up in the corner, where each powerful stroke of his tongue now banged it against the wall. Animal

His sleep was deep, with long, sensible dreams: next morning he woke as early as ever. Stilton lay beside him in a bar of pearly light. The kitten had already gone out. Animal X went to the door and looked into the garden, which was full of white mist and pale yellow sunshine.

'I always liked the dawn,' he decided quietly to himself. 'But today I like it more.'

The kitten had left a trail in the dewy grass to the bottom of the garden, then ploughed through the hedge into the pasture beyond, where it had sat grooming itself for a few minutes before making its way down to the little stream, to sniff around among the duck-droppings then wander off in the same direction as the current.

After a few hundred yards the stream entered a spacious water-meadow – low-lying, greyed with dewy spiderwebs, buttered with kingcups and dotted here and there by single tall thistles – on which the mist seemed to linger despite the growing warmth of the day. There it joined a broader, deeper stream, green, thick with weeds and apparently unmoving except where it plunged over a weir with a kind of mumbling roar. Above and beside the weir the air brightened in an arc of colour, as if the falling water had laundered the mist out of it. Everything was in sharp focus. Blue dragonflies hung and darted above the water. On the bank beside this theatre of light, its head cocked attentively to one side, sat the golden kitten, captivated by the fall and rush of the water, the broad silver weight of it as it poured over the weir, the creamy white standing wave from which broke suds of foam that were tossed up into the shiny air. Animal X went and sat companionably in the close-cropped turf nearby.

'What do you see?' he asked.

The kitten turned its face towards him. In its remaining eye gleamed a joy so quiet and pure it made him feel shy. An adult cat could only wince away from a look like that. When he was able to face it again, the kitten had forgotten he was there. It was too busy following the roar and plunge of the water across the weir, pausing to wonder how it folded itself over and danced into foam, then tilting its head assured him that they would stay together, the two of them waded off into the dew in the kitten's footsteps, unaware of the shadow that followed them across the meadows like a small cloud crossing the sun.

The kitten did calm down – though it took all day, and the day after that, and even then it seemed to keep a wary eye on Animal X and Stilton, and to walk a little apart from them. 'I don't know what I did,' thought Animal X, 'but I'd better be careful in future.' To Stilton, he said, 'That kitten wants friends, but it is too angry to let anyone near.'

'I would be angry too,' said Stilton.

Animal X stared at him. 'What do you mean?' he said.

But Stilton couldn't explain.

They walked for some days without anything happening, their course bounded by the water Animal X was reluctant to cross. The stream thickened and flexed its muscles. It wound through pastureland, or along the bases of gentle chalk hills, sometimes sharing the valley with a road. The three cats were never far from human beings – there was hardly a point in their journey when they were out of sight of the grey spire of a village church – but they kept to themselves. At midday they slept beneath a hedge; as dusk gathered, they found they were wading through chilly layers of mist as high as themselves, dammed into small fields like millponds. They froze at the call of an owl, the bark of a dog from a house in the moonlight; they caught the stark reek of a vixen and heard her cry later from the ridge for a mate. They ate what they could find, which was never enough, and they were glad of the hot afternoons.

While the golden kitten seemed to thrive on these hardships, Stilton grew increasingly ill and tired. His fur fell off in patches to reveal, smelly, yellowish and unhealed, the burns he had come by in the explosion. The burns frightened him, and he stopped cleaning himself rather than admit they were there. He rarely complained, but crouched listlessly in the open at night, his head turned away from the other cats, talking to himself as if he was back in the cabinet.

'I don't understand why.'

'To give myself a life,' said Stilton. 'I was born in that place. I was bred to go in the cabinets, I had no other purpose, and I've had no life but that until now, *but I don't mind*.' He said, 'I don't even mind if I die now. Do you want to know why?'

'Yes,' said Animal X.

Stilton looked up at the dark wall of trees behind them, the midges dancing above his head.

'Because I've been here and seen all this,' he said. 'And I've had a friend who took care of me.' His head drooped and he stared at the floor. 'I'm tired,' he said. 'You don't have to talk about cheese any more.' Then he said, 'Everyone minds dying. I don't know why I said that.'

Throughout this exchange, the golden kitten sat upright, gazing with a kind of ancient impassiveness out across the thistly pasture, the *tapetus lucidum* of its single eye blank and reflectant in the last eggshell-green light above the river. Who knew what it was thinking, or if it was thinking at all? Silently, it rose to its feet, stretched, and looked down at the sick cat. In that light it seemed bigger than itself. It stood over Stilton and began to lick him gently. Stilton offered up his tired face to the long, slow, careful passes of its tongue. He closed his eyes, and the kitten licked the mucus from them before it passed on to his ears, across the top of his head, and down his withered little sides and the burns that hurt him so much. After a moment, he sighed, and began to relax. The kitten gave a single, grunting purr which seemed to echo away across the fields. The stars appeared, one by one. A car whirred along some nearby lane. Suddenly it was pitch dark and off in the woods a brock was coughing. Stilton, who had begun to doze, woke up and shivered anxiously. But he was soon asleep again, and all that could be heard was the quiet rasp of the golden kitten's tongue.

'You were listening, then,' thought Animal X. 'I knew you were.'

pupil so that moonlight struck eerily off the milky-white membrane.

Her paws jerked.

Sealink was running. It was dark and icy cold. She was nowhere she recognized; nowhere she had even been, and certainly nowhere she wished to be again. The landscape through which she ran was featureless – the highway to end all highways – a black plain scoured by howling winds, winds that seemed designed to strip fur from skin and flesh from bone.

She had no clear idea why she ran, for the compulsion that drove her was deeper than thought. Something lay ahead of her, giving off a dull green light. No matter how hard she ran, this glow remained elusive, always the same distance away as it had been when she first sighted it, although her lungs burned from her exertions. At the same time, she sensed something behind her, and she knew by the way her spine prickled with heat that this something was gaining on her, inch by inexorable inch. She felt her lips draw back from her teeth with the effort, felt the desperate fluidity of her limbs as they gathered and flexed, gathered and flexed.

And then the voice was closer.

In the teeth of the wind, Sealink heard it.

It had a double tone, the first low and booming, like the drone of a pipe-organ, so deep that it shuddered in her bowels; the other was a voice she had heard before, vaguely familiar, but somehow distorted. It said:

'I am one who became two; I am two who become four; I am four who become eight; I am one more after that.' In and around the echo of these words, the demonic wind roared and subsided; roared and subsided. 'One more after that. After that. After that.'

'But you can't help us any more,' Sealink thought. 'I saw you die.'

Ahead, the glow deepened and spread. It rose from the dusky horizon like smoke from a bonfire and billowed towards the calico, who now stood rooted like a tree, her heart thumping in her chest. It twisted and twined for a

'Red sky in the morning, Great Cat's warning–'

Sealink stretched and yawned. She bent her head to groom her copious ruff, and at that moment a cry shattered the still air.

Red sped out of the hollow and leapt onto a fencepost. Every muscle taut with concentration, he stared into the distance, his tail lashing in agitation.

Sealink listened intently. The delay in the reception of the sound between one ear and the other enabled her to pinpoint the source of the cry with remarkable exactitude. She was on her feet at once, full of pent vigour.

'That's a cat in trouble, hon. Boneyard, north of Rampart.'

Red turned to stare in amazement. 'That's some pair of ears you got on you, sister.'

But Sealink was already running.

New Orleans, City of Good Times, City of Lost Care, City of Cats is also the City of the Dead. There are boneyards everywhere, each a miniature township dedicated to perpetual sleep. It might appear that these cemeteries are the true residential zones of the city; grimly enduring, elaborate and monumental, this is where the masons of Louisiana have lavished their craft; these are the areas that will outlast the charmingly distressed clapboard houses of the French Quarter and the shining modern towers of the Central Business District. Built above ground to defy the mighty river and the sucking drainage of the swamp, row upon row of windowless mausoleums line dusty, weed-strewn paths. Winged stone women hover massively among the tombs, suspended forever in watchful stasis. Cold white men, crowned with thorns, spread-eagled on crosses, appear suddenly at the intersections. Many gravesites are fenced around with iron stakes, fantastic and ornate, perhaps to ward the eye from their very functionality; but whether this gesture is designed to keep the dead in, or the living out, it is hard to determine. Walkers in these boneyards may sense they are being watched, not with the blind scrutiny of marble, but by quick, lambent eyes – little bundles of anima with sharp faces and slitted pupils.

Red shook his head.

Out of the corner of her eye, Sealink saw movement around the boneyard. The other ferals had started to creep out again, curiosity having got the better of their fear. They were painfully thin, like the cats outside the restaurant. Gaunt and hollow-eyed, their ribs showed through slack, dull coats like the staves of an old wooden boat. Underfed kittens huddled in unnatural silence in the long grass, the early-morning sun shining off their great round eyes.

Sealink whistled through her teeth. 'My, my. You guys all look sicker'n a dead dog.'

One of the ferals was bolder than the rest. He shouldered his way out into the open and stood there, his eyes watering in the light. 'What's it to you?'

'We heard this lady—' Red turned to the little bicolour. 'Hey, honey – what's your name?'

'Azelle.'

'We heard Azelle cry out – came to see if we could help.'

He turned to the bicolour, who was now keening wordlessly again, and, reaching up, licked her head in the most soothing way he knew.

At once, there was a movement beneath the palmettos. A little black and white cat with bright green eyes and a confident manner stepped out between the fronds and looked Red up and down appraisingly.

As if in reaction to this scrutiny, Red was all attention, his whiskers fanning the air. He dropped his forefeet back to the ground and stood there, his coat glowing in the ruddy light. Then he leaned forward. His features sharpened with sudden recognition.

'Téophine? Is that you?'

The little black-and-white smiled slyly. Then she opened her pink mouth wide and yelled, 'Hey, girls! He's a live one. Still got his *cojones*!'

At once there was a flurry of activity. From all over the boneyard, emaciated females emerged into the light, popping their heads out of broken tombs, stretching scrawny necks over their neighbours.

'Really? You ain't kiddin', Téophine?'

it is disturbed my morning; so I mean to find out exactly what caused Azelle here to howl so loud.'

The bicolour had stopped her melancholy circling and now sat, head down in exhausted defeat.

'They stole my kittens.'

Kittens. It all came back to kittens, again. Something dark and forbidding rose in her soul.

'Who stole your kittens?'

The bicolour mumbled something.

Sealink stared at her, aghast. 'You let other cats steal away your kittens?'

Azelle nodded. 'Weren't nothing I could do 'bout it.' She lifted mortified eyes. 'There were so many of them . . .'

Sealink was appalled. Furious, she turned to face the group. 'You let them take her kittens? You didn't try to help? What kind of cowards are you? Look at yourselves. Ain't you got no self-respect, to let yourselves get like this? I ain't ever seen so many filthy, starving cats, certainly not in the Big Easy. I seen a few on my travels – dying of cat flu in the slums of Calcutta; begging for scraps in the tourist joints of Skiathos; lining up for filthy leftovers in the arches of Coldheath: but you're the sorriest-looking bunch I ever did encounter – pardon my directness.'

This seemed to unleash a tide of explanation.

'They bin stealin' our kittens for weeks now – '

'These few are all that are left – '

An old grey cat bobbed its head out of an oven-tomb. 'Takin' them in broad daylight – '

Red stared around him. 'And y'all just let this happen?'

The old grey wheezed. It took a while for Red to realize it was laughing at him. 'Take a look at us, sonny. Y'all t'ink we any good for fightin'?'

Another voice. 'We all sick, boy.'

'Hell, we ain't just sick, we's dying.'

'Ain't got the strength we was born with.'

'Cain't barely stand up.'

A cacophony of voices.

'Ain't ate in a week – '

'People don't feed us no more.'

holding out in whatever way we can. There is no need to insult us in our last remaining domain.'

Sealink looked at her feet, for once in her life lost for words. Red stepped forward and bowed his head politely. 'Téophine – honey – I'm real sorry if we've given offence. Sealink here ain't exactly diplomatic—'

The calico opened her mouth to object, thought better of it, and closed it again.

'We only came here to help whoever was in trouble, but it looks to me as if that means all of you. We'd sure like to help in any way we can, but I have to say I'm findin' it kinda hard to take it all in. Perhaps we could sit down somewhere quiet and you could take us through things nice and slow?'

Téophine regarded him thoughtfully. 'Well, you're the only two able-bodied cats I seen in a long while, so I guess you could be useful—'

'Wait!'

A spindly-legged Siamese had pushed through the throng. Its little triangular head bobbed on its neck like a flower heavy with dew.

'I seen her yesterday.' The Siamese fixed Sealink with bright blue crossed eyes. 'I seen her dragging some great package up the street behind the French Market—'

'That's where the Bitch Queen hangs out—'

'Seen her go right on in there, and come out again, unscathed.'

Someone hissed.

'Spy!'

Another growled; others showed their teeth, yellow with rot. Even in their diseased state, they gave off an air of considerable menace.

Téophine put her head on one side. 'So. Why you hangin' out wit' Kiki La Doucette? What you bring her? What you got to say?'

The other ferals crowded around.

The calico drew herself up to her full, impressive height. 'I don't have to defend my actions to you. I was trading clawmarks with that old yellow queen before you was even born—'

As Sealink's eyes adjusted to the twilight of the tomb, she scrutinized the other occupants. Besides the little black-and-white, there were two other female cats – a scruffy tortoiseshell and a little colourpoint with a flattened face and matted coat – and the big striped male with the frilled ears. His masculine beauty was certainly marred now: not only by the fact that he'd been neutered, but also by a tail that hung at a curious angle, and the effects of the wasting sickness, which made his skin hang slack on dwindled muscles. All at once Sealink remembered her encounter with Blanco, the big white male outside the Farmer's Market whose skin had slipped away under her gripping teeth in such a disconcerting manner. She shuddered. Whatever it was these cats were suffering from, she sure didn't want to catch it.

Red was ensconced with Téophine in the far corner of the tomb, and the neutered male was watching possessively out of the corner of his eye. They had their heads down and were talking in low voices. Clearly catching up on old times, the calico thought waspishly. To distract herself from uncharitable thoughts, she turned to the striped cat. 'So tell me, honey: what the hell's been going on in this town?'

This animal, who had awarded himself the simple but grandiose title of the Hog, after the motorbike that had damaged his appendage, was obviously flattered by Sealink's interest. He dragged his eyes from the little black-and-white, and, with his fur puffed up and his ears pricked, started to talk:

'It bin happenin' for months now, lady. First of all people took grown cats, give 'em the operation, then let 'em go. Then when they take the ladies, they put 'em in a box and let 'em cry out till the little kitties come runnin' to find out why they momma's cryin'. Then they takes the kitties. To start wit' they just put a needle in the kitties, then bring 'em back, give 'em food, too. The next thing we knows, the Pestmen comes with their boxes and kitties started to disappear in they ones and twos. Then it was whole litters, out playin' in the street – next t'ing, they gone – shoom – like they was never there.'

At the other end of the tomb, Téophine's head shot up. 'I heard that name, but not for some time.'

'How about the Majicou?'

'We heard the Majicou was dead.'

Sealink considered for a moment, decided against venturing the details. 'That's what I heard, too.'

'Do you know the Mammy?'

Sealink wrinkled her brow. 'I remember the name.'

'She used to be the guardian round these parts,' offered the tortoiseshell.

'Can't she help? Seems to me you guys could do with some guardianship.'

Téophine shook her head. 'She ain't here no more – she's way out in the old swamps – in the bayous.'

'So?'

'It's a long way, and it ain't safe.'

Sealink sensed an adventure, a new kind of journey, one with a clear goal and simple motives; a journey, moreover, that would take her out of a city which she had once loved and which now seemed irrevocably poisoned. 'Tell me where to find her and I'll go talk to the Mammy. Someone's got to do something round here before the whole thing goes to hell in a handcart.'

Téophine's knowledge as to the whereabouts of the Mammy amounted to little more than an awareness of a seldom-used wild road that supposedly led out to the Bayou Gros Bon Ange from the seedy end of Iberville, but she and Red insisted on accompanying the calico at least that far. Red had offered to journey with her into the ancient backwaters, but Sealink could tell from the looks he and the little black-and-white exchanged that his heart was not in it. For a second she felt desperately jealous.

'Still,' she muttered, as they trotted down Dauphine, '*ménage à trois* just ain't my scene.'

Towards the corner of Bienville they found a little ginger and white cat with a pink velour collar wandering disconsolately up and down.

Sealink approached it.

He unravelled a wide-meshed net and with some expertise cast it out into the shadow where she cowered. At once there was pandemonium. Téophine shrieked and fought the net but the more she struggled, the more the net tangled her limbs.

'Téo, no!'

Spitting and howling, Red sped up the road towards her, a streak of orange fury. He launched himself at the net-man, fangs bared.

Sealink stared, horrified. Then she, too, fled up the street: in the opposite direction.

She ran and ran. She ran until her lungs burned and the pads of her paws felt raw and bruised. And, as she ran, the blood roared in her ears, roared and thundered like a great, dark storm until she could almost feel the fingers of a gigantic black hand reaching out to break the green-gold of a symbol that hung before her like the promise of hope, and she knew that she would have to run for ever to evade it; and that even if she ran from it for ever the world would eventually be eaten away around her so that she would exist in a terrible void, alone save for the hand and the words that had reverberated through her dream; and at last she stopped, her chest heaving, her eyes watering with fear, and shame and horror washing hot and heavy through her veins.

What had she done? She had deserted a cat she had come to think of as more than a friend; and a brave, sick feral who needed all the help she could get. She had run and left them to whatever fate awaited them in the hands of the men in black overalls, men who could only be the Pestmen the boneyard cats had spoken of in hushed tones. Another betrayal.

The image of the pink velour collar on the ground returned sharply to her mind's eye: a terrible image of innocence traduced.

What was happening in this city? What was happening to her? Had she, too, caught the wasting sickness the feral cats suffered from? Had it perhaps attacked not her flesh, but

XI

The Symbol

The Queen licked her paws for a moment.

'It was the water again after that,' she said. 'Cold currents. The bony, hollow halls of the ocean.'

She sighed.

'I did not find my children,' she said softly. 'But if nothing else, I have seen the Nile.'

It was so quiet in the oceanarium that Tag could hear waves falling on the beach half a mile away. For a moment, he imagined them as the breakers of another, gentler, sea. A dreamy warmth stole over him, full of the life and bustle of strange cities, smells of spices, the taste of things he had never eaten before. He shook himself.

'But what about *Cy*?' he said. 'If the Great Ray brought all three of you home, where is she?'

The King and Queen looked at one another.

'Tag, we don't know,' admitted Ragnar.

'Goodbye for now,' the tabby had said, looking up at the King and Queen in the hard actinic glare of the aquarium lamp. 'It's Thousand Island Fever for us, now you guys are safe back from the Egypt package. It's activity holidays and all, and, you know, reckless navigation. We got more stuff to do, me and this Ray-guy.' With that, tabby and fish had vanished in a lazy swirl of black water, leaving the amazed royal couple to stare down into the tank, which now seemed shadowy and unbounded, bigger inside than out. For a long time afterwards, the Queen had thought she could still hear Cy's voice, saying, in a kind of receding echoic whisper, 'We got more things to see!'

Tag was quiet for a long time when he heard this.

'She's very much her own cat, of course,' he said eventually.

'Gone out for chips,' he suggested. 'It will be tomcats next,' he predicted placidly. The Queen gave him an old-fashioned look. 'Oh, that is one bad daughter,' he said.

'I wonder where she learns it?' Pertelot enquired.

She said to Tag, 'Don't worry so, Mercury. You can't look after her all the time.'

'You don't understand,' said Tag. 'I mean I really have—' Appalled by their faith in him, he found he couldn't continue. 'Look,' he said, 'she's probably down at the Beach-O-Mat now. I'll go and fetch her. No, no: you stay here.' And he went off thinking miserably, 'Now I've lied to them, too.'

Out on the cobbles in the quiet night, he turned right instead of left, and soon stood on a wooden bench on the clifftop above the village. He welcomed the chilly onshore breeze, with its odours of iodine and salt. The cottages fell away from him among flights of steps, narrow alleys, stone-cropped walls. The big sky was planished with moonlight, the ocean a litter of small waves breaking Chinese-white on charcoal. Far out on the horizon, the inshore fishing-boats were at work in a scatter of lights. He imagined the fish-ermen drawing in the nets, water pouring over the decks, then the slithering silver haul spilt out, mixed with shells, starfish, weeds and bits of plastic rubbish. But that only made him think of Cy, eyeing him with her head on one side and saying, 'Tag, we got *stargazey pie*!' She loved fish, and now she had gone off with one. Suddenly, he couldn't bear to have lost two cats in one night. He jumped off the bench and ran down the hill to Cy's bus shelter of choice, where he encountered two or three hard-favoured village toms, boasting away the midsection of the night as they waited for the fishing-boats to return. When they saw who he was they quietly took themselves elsewhere. He was rather hurt by this, nevertheless watched them intently as they backed away, as if to catch something unawares in their blank, reflectant eyes. He sat there for some time. After an hour or so, mist formed in the bay and sent cold fingers the colour of poached egg-white up across the water and into the town.

mean, stranger than it usually is over there. It was cold and damp where I was, like a lot of empty passageways going off in all directions. Water was dripping all around me, but I knew it was a kind night out in the real world, the sky clear, the fields giving up the heat of the day. I could almost hear the mice, cupped in nests of warm grass: yet there I stood, with this raw damp cold in the bones. Tag – ' she stared intently at him, as if she would recognize an answer whether he spoke or not ' – have you ever felt as if your life was draining out of you? As if you were poisoned, or – ' she thought for a moment ' – *fading out* somehow?' She shivered with the memory of it. 'I'll tell you, I was a scared kitten at that point. I was lost. I was cold. I was going to sleep without wanting to. If you had turned up to show me the way home at that moment I just wouldn't have had the energy to take it.'

She eyed him shrewdly.

'Of course, you didn't,' she reminded him. 'Turn up, I mean.'

Tag decided to ignore this.

'Lassitude,' he said. 'Feelings of vagueness. I've never heard of anything like it. But there were many things I never had a chance to learn. And then again, perhaps it is something quite new.'

'Nice to get the views of an expert,' said Leonora. 'Everything you say makes me feel a lot better.'

'No-one can know everything,' Tag said.

'I'm finding that out. Have I hurt your feelings again?'

'A little. What did you do next?'

'Everything had gone grey. All the life, the beauty, the worth had gone out of everything,' said Leonora. 'I don't want that!' she said. 'I'm young, I want the world to be worth having! So I danced. I made a dance for myself, and I was in it. Look.' She jumped down out of the tumble-drier and danced on the laundromat floor, less, Tag thought, to show him than to remind herself. 'Very slowly at first. Point one toe, place one foot. Very slow, very measured steps, no jumps or pounces. Then faster, faster, until I felt strong.' She laughed. 'You see?' she said. 'Like this,' she said. She

The moon glinted off rictus grin and snaggle-teeth. A low, penetrating yowl issued forth, to curl over the spoiled lawn, briefly lick Leonora's bones, then float away across the surrounding streets. Almost at once, three or four brutalized-looking tomcats appeared on the rotten board fence at the bottom of the garden. After a brief conference, they jumped down as one and swept off into the Midland night with Kater Murr at their head.

'Looking for any kind of trouble,' thought Leonora; and her sympathy went out to the innocents they met.

As soon as she was sure they weren't coming back she scampered over and popped her head through the cat flap. The house rang with Kater Murr's smell, suspended like a foul bell in the latent heat of the stairs. By fits and starts, in the jangling moonlight-and-dark, she made her way up to the ramshackle gallery at the very top of the house. She peered round the door of each empty room on the way. On the second-floor landing an open window banged to and fro. She froze. She ran. 'Take care, Leonora,' she told herself, just to hear a familiar voice. 'Now this way. Quick now! Make no sound!'

Moonlight filled the Library of Uroum Bashou, pouring in so brightly that she could make out the black lines of print on the pages of the opened books. There were dark bars and smudges of shadow across the dusty floor, the dry, faded wainscoting, the otiose velvet cushions: the darkest of them was the Librarian himself, a skinny black comma (as he himself would have said) in the Great Text of Life. Spread out in front of him on the dusty floor – as if he could read them too – the remains of a pigeon made a scribble of bones and feathers. The room was full of a strange, thready humming. Broken quarter-tones rose and fell. Leonora cocked her head and laughed softly. Uroum Bashou had recently finished his dinner and was purring to himself as he washed in the moonlight.

'This was all very ill-advised,' said Tag.

'I know,' said Leonora. 'And don't think I wasn't nervous. I was. But you know, he's not such a bad old cat.

He made an impatient motion. 'Then there is nothing to read,' he concluded.

'Wait,' she told him.

And, with considerable concentration, because cats do not often try to do this, she used her front left paw to trace in the dust the symbol she had seen in the sea-cave below Tintagel Head:

As soon as Uroum Bashou saw what she was trying to do, he became violently excited. 'It is a book of the floor!' he cried, his reedy voice full of delight. 'It is a book of dust!' His dignity fled him, to reveal the kitten beneath. All the young Handkerchief's intellectual delight, his raging curiosity, escaped for a moment the ponderous academic skin of the Elephant. He purred and chirruped. He jumped back up onto his pillows and stood with his knotted tail quivering in the air, reaching down every so often to tap at her paws with his own.

'Yes, yes, yes!' he said.

'Not clear enough!' he said.

He said, 'Try again! Try again!'

So Leonora tried again, her foreleg quivering with the effort and oddness of the motion. And then again.

'Bigger. Bigger! Uroum Bashou has never read the dust before.'

As soon as they had a symbol he could work with, the Reading Cat became thoughtful, and he seemed to forget Leonora altogether. 'Mm,' he said. Slowly, paw by paw, as if he was stalking a mouse, he came down off his cushions to look at it from another angle, then another. He introduced his whiskers to the air above it. He wandered off sniffing aimlessly at the tumbled heaps of books: then pounced without warning, scraping and scratting with his forepaws until he found the volume he wanted. This he

In the Beach-O-Mat, Tag asked Leonora, 'And what had he found, the Reading Cat?'

'A single book, very old, its pages made of something thick, yellow and fragile which had been mounted on ordinary paper. He thought it came from Egypt; and that it might have started life as something else, only to be made into a book later, to preserve it. There, among many others, was the symbol! It was faded and rather oddly proportioned, but I recognized it immediately.'

'Ah,' said Tag.

He leaned forward suddenly.

'What else?' he urged.

'He said that there was no explanatory text. He said that symbols like this appear very early in the history of men and cats, though never earlier than something he called "the Missing Dynasty". He said they are associated with the celebration, or "bringing down", of a goddess.'

'And?'

'He thought for a long time and then said that he was sure he remembered the Old Majicou asking him the same question.'

'Nothing about the Golden Cat? Nothing about kittens?'

'No,' said Leonora.

Tag sighed impatiently.

'Then we are still no further forward,' he said. He stared out of the laundromat window at the mist and the sea.

'Don't you want to hear what happened next?'

When he was reading, Uroum Bashou customarily used his paw to keep his place. As soon as he removed it from the pages of the very old book, tensions in the binding caused them to turn over at random, like a deck of cards spilled upon a polished floor. When this process finished, another symbol was revealed:

$$\odot$$

Leonora touched the book. It was warm. She felt a faint, electrical sensation. The flutter and whirr of the turning she went. (Where was she going to hide? There was nowhere he couldn't find her. She would end up like an air-dried pigeon in the base of a cupboard.) It was light for a little way, then dark to the second landing. She could hear her own breath so loud she never heard his. And, anyway, how could it have been him? Without any warning at all there was something huge and made of metal, hurling itself up the stairs towards her with hallucinatory speed, in a rage at being so confined, its broad brassy chops full of teeth promising her death every time the stairwell brushed its ribs on either side. Its bared red tongue was bigger than her head! Its *face* was a foot and a half wide and its claws were taking chunks out of the fibrous old wooden risers as it came. Suddenly it was on the landing with her, pacing up and down, giving a great coughing snarl, weaving to and fro in the slippery light. Up close, the metal appeared to give way to fur, coarse and orange. With every bunch-and-pull of its huge muscles, violent markings of a slightly lighter colour roiled down its sides like painted flames. It stank of ammonia, pheromones, death. It lifted its head and roared.

Leonora backed away.

The open landing window banged to and fro above her. She jumped out of it.

For a while she seemed to float. The night air pressed up against her. She turned over and over as she fell, so that first the sky, then the street passed slowly through her field of vision. Below her was a basement area with its pointed railings. Further out, parked cars. She thought she saw three or four shadows milling about down there between the wheels; but, by the time she could look again, the street was empty, lunar-silent. Suddenly, everything speeded up. She looked down. 'The railings!' she thought. 'The railings!' Then they were past, and she had landed heavily on a pile of wet cardboard boxes and plastic garbage bags, liberally spattered with the produce of the pigeons which lived on the window-ledges above. The breath went out of her, along with every-thing else.

When she woke up, she felt light-headed with her own luck. Her first thought was: 'Still alive!' Her first instinct afourche, and Barataria eke out a tenuous existence amongst a maze of channels and quagmires, abandoned river channels, or bayous – dead-end cricks and sloughs, marshes, abandoned ponds and oxbow lakes; an impossible place to map; an easy place to be lost in; a breeding-ground for a billion insects, for fish with teeth as sharp as rats' fangs, and for creatures seeking larger prey . . .

And all throughout this five-thousand-year period, and well beyond that meaningless man-made time-scheme, the wild roads of the animals of the South have wound their way across and through this area, oblivious to the temporary changes inflicted upon it by humankind. The territory into which the wild roads debouch is still the treacherous, mystical landscape recognized, and avoided, by most humans; but the wild roads have traditionally offered safe passage through this quaggy labyrinth for those cats and other creatures willing to use them for their journeys. Until now.

When Sealink entered, in a state of blind panic and horror, the wild road whose entrance lay between Iberville and Bienville streets in the old French Quarter of the city of New Orleans, she sensed that something fundamental in the nature of the roads had changed since last she had set foot upon them. For a start, all was dark, and the compass winds which all cats know to be not only themselves, but a gale of souls, were silent.

Where were the ghost cats?

It was too quiet.

She raised her great head. The air inside this highway was sluggish and stale, as if the swamps were extending their domain into the very heart of the city.

Perhaps, then, it was this road alone that was affected and, as Téophine had said, no-one used it any more, perhaps not even the shades of earlier cats. But if the road was long abandoned by living and dead alike, it would soon cease to exist. And if that happened, she would have a long and dangerous journey through the bayous. Better run, then, and make use of it while she could. Great paws striking and flexing with every footfall, Sealink let the

and walked up past it, along a tidy gated road between cow-pastures the broad gentle slopes of which were sprinkled with buttercups and dotted here and there with clumps of dark green thistle. Though the sky was blue and tranquil, it already had a metallic sheen, a promise of heat at noon. A few crows circled lazily in the shimmering air somewhere up ahead.

'Such a beautiful day,' said Leonora.

She said, 'Here we are!'

The road made its way into a little intimate fold of land: stopped. At first, Tag couldn't make anything of what he saw. The building had been split as if by a single clean stroke from some vast cleaver, its two halves then settling slightly, still joined at the base but leaning away from each other.

'Stay here, Leonora.'

Cautiously, Tag approached one of the shattered windows. He sniffed, jumped up; peered inside. Loops of black cable hung down where the ceiling had buckled and split. Everything inside had been smashed beyond identification. The floor was thick with bits of wood, bent metal, warped plastic panels, stinking of char, coated with plaster-dust that days of rain had turned into a kind of cement. He identified a table, which seemed to have been thrown bodily against the wall; a white human garment with one sleeve torn off. Among the disordered objects, silent cats lay in windrows. The air over them was infused with the sour simple smell of death.

'Leonora, don't—' Tag began.

Too late. She had jumped up beside him and was staring in.

'Who would do this?' she whispered.

She stared at him.

'Who is doing this to us? The wild roads are spoiled. Cats are dying everywhere. Tag, I was so happy to be home this morning. But nothing is what it promised to be!'

Before he could answer, she had jumped down and begun to sniff her way between the bodies. He knew what she was looking for, but he hadn't the heart to help her. After a little while, he heard her say, as if to herself, 'I don't want to be a kitten any more. It isn't worth it.'

powerful chemicals of her primal self absorb and dissipate her doubts and fears.

So it was that some time later an observer might have seen a rare sight: a great, striped cat emerging as if from nowhere into the fronded shade of a flooded forest. Luckily for Sealink, however, there were no observers here, at least no humans sighting down their hunting rifles for prey – for, if there had been at that precise moment, they might have bagged the trophy of a lifetime and started a fervour of debate about the natural life of the Louisiana swamplands.

Now, just a second or two later, all anyone would have seen was a much smaller member of the *felidae* family: albeit a large and well-furred calico cat, its patches of orange and black and white now a far more random and less terrifying camouflage arrangement in that strange twilight than her wild-road pelt.

If there were no humans here, of other life there was no lack. Where the highway had been eerily silent, the bayou was bursting with sound. An extraordinary din of life filled the heavy air – chirrups and peeps, buzzing and rasping and whining – heralding the presence of cigarriens and chiggers; crickets and gnats and ticks, and a thousand bird-voiced tree frogs.

Sealink stared at this unfamiliar new environment. Channels, viscous and bubbling with gas, punctuated by islands of floating water hyacinth and natural levees bound together by mud and mangrove roots like claws. Beyond, a tangle of willow and hickory, dog-oak and sweetgum and myrtle, all swathed in trailing beards of grey Spanish moss. Webs inhabited by spiders as large as her head spanned the branches of a nearby cypress.

Sealink shuddered. Where the hell was she to find Mammy Lafeet amongst all this chaos? She turned a tight circle. In particular, how was she to find the Mammy without getting her feet wet?

At that moment there was a loud whirring and a flash of neon green-and-blue and suddenly a pair of large, prismatic eyes were hovering just in front of the calico's nose, borne heard it say something. Then it veered off into a stand of willows, and, even as the calico turned to watch it, it was back, its whirring and buzzing even more insistent. This time, it clipped her nose with a wing-tip, a featherlight brush, and a minute, tinny voice sounded in the back of her ear:

'*Follow.*'

Sealink shook her head as if to dislodge a flea. She must be going crazy. Still, why not? She'd fit right in here. Feeling dislocated from her species and her own experience, the calico made a leap from the floating island on which she stood to the more substantial ground where the willows grew. Ahead of her, the dragonfly dipped and darted; and Sealink followed.

A short while later, led far into the swampland, Sealink was distracted by an interesting smell. It was quick and sharp and warm-blooded, and not far away. The calico had never been the most skilled of wild hunters: travelling with the Queen of Cats across the desolate moors of Cornwall they might well have starved had it not been for Pertelot's unexpected talent. Give Sealink a trash can, however, and she would rip the life out of it in seconds; but there weren't too many of those great symbols of civilized life around here, and, not having eaten for hours, she was, she realized suddenly, ravenous. Let the dragonfly hover for a moment: she'd inspect the food-source.

Some yards to the left, beneath a stand of mallows, there sat a fat rat. Sealink had seen others of its kind in her past, but right now its precise taxonomy seemed unimportant. It sat there, apparently petrified by her presence, the moon-light glinting off its beady black eyes, exuding a fine, strong reek of well-salted food. The calico, delighted with her luck, squatted into stalking mode, waggled her ample bottom until she had the beast properly sighted, and launched herself into the mallows. From its lair, the nutrea rat watched her with alarm, then, as soon as she leapt – a great, ungainly mass of fur and claws – shot neatly into the water.

Sealink paced up and down the bank, hoping that it might

tall white flowers of an arrowroot, a cricket frozen against the bark of a live oak; but when something shifted in her peripheral vision, it seemed to come from the dark hollow between two logs, and, even with her night sight working overtime, she couldn't quite make out the originator of the movement. She stepped closer, her paws making no sound on the soft leaf-mould underfoot.

Then, suddenly, something shone out of the gloom.

An eye!

She sprang back, swallowing a cry. It was a big, golden eye, glowing in the darkness. With a sigh of relief she recognized the vertical black slit of another cat's pupil.

'Mammy Lafeet!'

The relief was immense. It washed through her like hot milk.

'You sure take some findin', Momma. Can't imagine why anyone should want to hide themselves away from civilization to such an extent – not that it's all that civilized back there at the moment. Which is why I need to talk to you. But first things first, eh, podna? After that trek I sure could do with some nourishment, y'know honey. You don't happen to have a little something I could chew on while we talk, do you?'

The eye regarded Sealink steadily.

Then, even as she was congratulating herself on locating the Mammy at the dead of night in the midst of this fearsome wilderness, the eye blinked, and the relief curdled in her stomach.

The eye had blinked sideways, like a camera shutter.

Sealink's mind scrambled to make sense of this observation. Perhaps the Mammy was suffering from some kind of optical disorder. Perhaps she was lying with her head on one side. Perhaps—

Then another detail insinuated itself neatly into this rickety structure of rationalizations. The pupil that split the golden eye was the narrowest of lines, yet she could feel her own pupils distended to full, black circles in this darkness.

Not the Mammy, then.

Not even a cat.

'Er, not right now, babe. Maybe some other time?'

The grin widened a crack.

'That's a shame, *chérie*. I have a nook down there that's just your size. Unfortunately I visited my store only a short while ago and gorged myself on the most succulent little white-tailed deer you could ever imagine. *Ciel!*' It smacked its chops together appreciatively. 'Sheer bliss.' It pushed itself up on its stubby arms so that Sealink could observe the great swell of its scaly belly. 'Indeed, I am so full it hurts. I couldn't fit in another morsel. *Vraiment, c'est dommage*, it is a profound pity, *mon ange*: it has been such a long time since I had the pleasure of partaking of the subtle flesh of a feline friend.'

Sealink decided to push her luck.

'You wouldn't happen to know where I might find a very old, and I'm sure extremely stringy, feline known as the Mammy Lafeet, would you?'

The alligator laughed, a strange creaking sound like a dead branch sawing in the wind. 'Even creatures of the greatest age and gristle become tender when subjected to my fine Louisiana marinade, *chérie*.'

'Oh.'

'Although I pride myself on being a true *gourmand* – ' he leered ' – even *I* must draw the line somewhere. And the Mammy has, how you say, "laid the bones upon me". I eat her: I die of the bellyache. This is what she promises me. Not a friendly gesture in this cruel and hostile world. Not the sort of hospitality one would expect from a neighbour. *Alors*, I think she is not to my taste, *pour le déjeuner*, or as company! You however . . .' he paused.

The calico watched him distrustfully, flight plans formulating swiftly in her head.

'. . . may keep on walking. She's somewhere out there.' He waved a tiny, clawed hand airily. '*Eh bien*, it is time now for my swim. Life on the levee is hard and lonely. Do visit with me again, *bébé*, when you are passing in this direction.' He finished with a toothy grin, 'I will be sure to make you welcome, *chérie*.'

Then, with a slither and a great splash, the alligator

that Sealink could barely catch it, *'Not called* fishbait.*'*

That was it. She was definitely losing it. She was lost in the most horrible wilderness she could ever have imagined; an alligator had nearly had her as a postprandial treat, and now she was getting lectured by a dragonfly!

'Mammy close. Follow now. Pay attention this time.'

Sealink sighed and followed as instructed.

The dead time between day and night, those two or three hours that precede the rising of the sun, when humans lie in the deepest trenches of their sleep and diurnal beings take to their burrows, is the time when the *felidae* and other creatures of the night tend to be at their most active and acute.

Sealink, however, preferred to sleep at this time, particularly when there was no food to be had. It took her mind off things. She would also have been the first to concede that full dark could make her a little edgy. She was not, therefore, in the best frame of mind for her next discovery.

On the barely discernible track along which the dragonfly led her there had been at intervals a number of partially rotted and foul-smelling objects which might once have been small rodents or reptiles. A few yards further and there was a small turtle shell, minus its occupant. Then cat and dragonfly rounded a bend and emerged out into a small clearing, in the middle of which lay two large identically round stones like garden ornaments, and something else . . .

This object stood higher than her head and seemed to soak up all the available starlight, which it gave back in a great albescent glow, illuminating its component parts: an intricate, obsessive jigsaw of skulls and ribcages, spinal columns and hip-bones; fishbones and rigid claws; open beaks and empty orbital sockets – the ghastly remains of a thousand soulless bodies.

Sealink stared, for a moment trapped motionless in her native curiosity. She sniffed at the bone-mountain. Then she tapped it cautiously with a paw. At once, the entire heap collapsed, sending tiny skulls and skeletons skittering down upon her, as cold and smooth and light as a shower of dead beetles.

Mammy Lafeet must finally be close by; rapidly followed by disorientation and self-doubt.

'Who the hell are you and what are you talking about?'

'How do we know this isn't a test?' It sidled closer, snuffling. Sealink put a paw out defensively. Her claws popped from their sheaths and gleamed in the cold light.

'Back off, buddy.' Definitely not as fearsome as the alligator. She decided to take a stern tone with it. 'Look, I'm here to see the Mammy. I ain't here to play games. Please go find her and tell her she has a visitor.'

'You knocked over our pile.'

The first guard now had its back to Sealink and its companion and was trundling disconsolately around the debris, gathering skulls into one heap, fishbones into another.

'Er, yes. Sorry.'

'Took us ages, that did.'

It started to stack bones haphazardly. The new foundations reached a height of perhaps five inches, tottered and collapsed. At once the second guard waddled over, muttering disapprovingly, 'Not like that. Don't you ever learn? Start with *these* . . .'

She'd get no sense out of these guys. Shaking her head, Sealink left them to it.

Some yards beyond the clearing, the calico found herself at the water's edge again and out in clear, if stifling, air. A dull glow in the eastern sky announced that dawn might not be far off, for which she found she was truly grateful. She sat down to await the new day, staring out over the spreading ripples of rising fish. Eventually, new light lent colour to her strange surroundings. It infused the pink of the mallow flowers and the lilac of the water hyacinths. It delineated the leaves of the dog-oak and the fronds of the buckler fern and crept into the duckweed on the surface of the bayou to light it to a phosphorescent, neon green. It marked out a snapping turtle on a rotting log, long neck stretched out to catch the first of the rays, his mouth as leathery and puckered and downturned as that of a toothless old man.

She cleared her throat, started again. 'Folks mostly call me Sealink. After a boat I once came in on.'

'Sealink.' The old cat savoured the word in her soft Creole. 'It is good that we trade names with one another, chile. It is a matter of trust, *hein*? Cats' names are important: they are words of power. So, Sealink. A traveller. One who bridges many worlds. *Un voyageur*. A cat bearing news and a gift of gold who crosses oceans – an ocean of salt, and of fire.'

'Fire?' Sealink was alarmed.

'I have myself passed through fire. I have smelled the smell of fire,' pronounced Eponine in a singsong voice. She turned a serene face to her visitor. *'Viens.'*

Without checking to make sure the calico was following she disappeared abruptly into the dense undergrowth and, stepping neatly between aerial roots and knots of vegetation, made her way unerringly to another, hidden shore of the bayou, and the upturned hull of a small wooden boat, its timbers weathered to silver by the passing seasons.

All around the skiff lay an assortment of tiny bones and feathers, some arranged in curious patterns, others scattered as if at random, all making a stark contrast against the peaty ground. The Mammy sat down and began to pat some loose bones into a small pile. She looked up at the calico and her mouth parted to reveal a few sharp, white teeth in what might have been a smile; or maybe it was just senility. Sealink found it hard to tell.

'*Eh bien, cher*: you made a long journey down old roads to get here. You taken your life like a mouse in your mouth – *une souris dans ta bouche* – and held it tight but gentle through fear and peril. You been through hazard to reach me, *alors, je pense que t'as bonne raison*. I figure you got just cause. And even though you ain't brung the Mammy no *cadeau*, because I sense you got troubles, I'm gonna allow you to ax me three silver questions, and in exchange I give you three silver answers.'

The calico looked bewildered.

'Honeychile, you gets to ax three questions. Don't you ever listen to no stories?'

Monsignor Gutbag: the very name the dragonfly had applied to the beast. A deep furrow scored Sealink's forehead, but she kept her lip buttoned.

Eponine regarded her through slitted eyes. A tiny buzzing sound rose from her throat, followed by a tiny voice barely more than a reverberation.

A gasp of amazement escaped from the calico. It was an uncanny piece of mimicry. But how could a cat use an insect thus? Sealink had the sense of being teased.

'I have my ways. Proxies can be very useful to a cat wit' bones as old as mine, but I got to take what I can – flies, armadillos . . . T'ey ain't too smart, but when you stuck out here you don't get much choice. Even so,' she fixed Sealink with a gimlet stare, 'it takes two to work: one to guide and one to follow; and if the one who follows don't pay attention – *bouff!*' She expelled a great cheekful of air that bespoke irritation and waste. 'You take my meanin'? So when you ax your t'ree questions, *cher*, you listen real good, 'cos when da bones talk t'ey can be real obscure.'

So saying, the Mammy retrieved a collection of bones from beneath the timbers of the boat. They lay in morning light, pale against the dark ground.

'Touch da bones, chile.'

Sealink sniffed at them but they gave back no clue of their origin. They looked smooth and polished with wear, their ends yellowing with age.

'Touch da bones.' The Mammy's voice was suddenly fierce. 'Touch dem and t'ink about your questions. Concentrate wit' the wildest part of yourself. Make dem a part of you. Believe in da bones.'

Sealink tried to clear her mind of all but those questions that demanded answers, but her thoughts milled about subversively – thoughts of times long gone, pointless memories of meals she had eaten, places she had been. She remembered eating noodles with Tom Yang outside a Bangkok temple; sharing fried chicken with the cats on the boardwalk. She remembered mates she had taken and friends she had made. She remembered Cy and Pertelot and an old seacat by the name of Pengelly and how he had she had seen shining in a silver cat's eyes had found a home inside her, and she knew what her first question must be. She opened her eyes and stared at the Mammy.

'Eponine. Tell me: what was gone so wrong in the world that the cats of the city are sick and persecuted?'

The Mammy closed her eyes and fell amongst the bones. She rubbed her cheek-glands upon them. She rolled onto her back and twisted her spine against them. She leapt to her feet and danced upon them, and Sealink had a fleeting memory of the jig that she and Baron Raticide had shared down on the Moonwalk only a few days before. Then the Mammy scooped up the bones and juggled them with clever paws. Balanced between momentum and gravity for a moment they hung, freighted with magic; then fell in a series of dry clicks to the ground, where they made a curious, disjointed creature, a creature with three legs and a single round of vertebra for a head.

Eponine looked at the pattern the fall of bones had made, then jumped away from the symbol as if scalded. She started to murmur to herself, agitated little grunts and grimaces; but the calico could make out not a word.

At last, Sealink could bear it no longer. 'What do the bones say?'

The Mammy stared right through her. Then in the strange singsong voice she had adopted earlier, she announced, *'Dans le coeur . . . Isaac le Noir et le Chat Noir . . . la danse macabre. Bon 'ti ange et gros 'ti ange, ils dansent toujours. Ils mangent le monde jusqu'à la mort . . . Les rues sauvages se meurent . . . Ça ne finit pas . . . Tempora mutantur . . . Et les rêves—'*

'Speak English!' Sealink was beside herself with frustration. But the Mammy was oblivious.

'Les trois. Les trois sont perdus. Ils doivent être retrouvés. C'est tout ou rien. All or nothing.'

Now the Mammy fell silent. Sealink stared at her. 'What? I don't understand – I don't speak that stuff. C'mon, be fair. I got the "all or nothing" bit, and I can kinda see it's a desperate situation out there, but that sure don't help me *understand* things.'

inconsequential in comparison to the first, but even so –

'What was in the *cadeau* I brought to Kiki La Doucette?'

The Mammy regarded the calico with suspicion.

'You a friend of Kiki's?'

'Er, no . . . not exactly.'

'Because if you are, *ça finit ici* – it ends here.'

'I'm not, truly.'

Eponine dealt the bones again. This time she cast them high in the air, and when they came down they had formed a rough circle with a single dot of a bone in its centre.

'Gold. It is the symbol for gold.'

'Oh.'

So there it was. She had dragged a lump of gold through the streets of the French Quarter. But what cat would have a use for inert metal? Her brain struggled with metaphors, then gave up. She'd had an answer in plain English, and she was still no closer. So much for her attempt to seek wisdom, to find the knowledge that would free the cats of New Orleans from the strange affliction that had them in its grasp; so much for understanding why the humans of the city had started to hate them so. Téophine would be disappointed. Téophine, and Red.

A twists of the stomach, a flush of shame. After the Pestmen had done with them, there would *be* no Téophine and Red to explain all this to . . .

Her last question. Giving up all pretence at selflessness, Sealink decided on this: 'I had five kittens once upon a time. I believe I know about four of 'em. But if the last is still alive, where can I find it?'

For the final time, Mammy Lafeet cast the bones. They landed all over the place. She shuffled around them, putting her head on one side then the other. She screwed her face up as if trying to focus on something very small. At last she pronounced:

'Two are with the Great Cat
Two are with La Mère.
The fifth lies between.'

'Look. I know you can only tell me what the bones tell you, but at least try to give me some help here,' Sealink queening around callin' herself La Mère? I know her poison better than most. I should; for I bore her. *Elle est la mienne.* I am her mother.'

at random, blundering through the tangled undergrowth and calling, 'Stilton! Stilton!' The voices in his head made it impossible to tell if Stilton had answered. More by luck than judgement he got back on the nearest ride and ran until he burst out of the woods. There was the river again, and water-meadows, and a village. Black birds flew up from the yews around the village church, and began to circle through the grey sheets of rain. The whole sky seemed to be running and melting into liquid around them. They knew he was there—

'The crows!' thought Animal X. 'The crows!'

He saw Stilton and the kittens come out of the woods and look at him as if he was mad.

'Run!' he called.

He saw the light come out of the woods after them and flicker about their heads. It glittered and crackled. Animal X winced away. He flattened his ears and ran towards the river. All around him it was water. Behind him he could hear the green fuse burning. Above him the great black birds swung and banked, shrieking and cawing. He shook his head to clear it. He could hear too many shrieks for the number of crows.

'Run!' he thought. 'Run!'

Halfway across, the fuse burned out, and there was a great soft silent explosion in the woods. Flames sprang up in the meadow around him, turning immediately into little fires which seemed to burn without any fuel. Animal X ran harder. Then he saw the river in front of him. Caught like that between the fire and the water, he was branded with awe and fear. The birds seemed to gather above him. Their cries redoubled. They were ready to swoop down. He knew he couldn't cross water, even on a bridge: to enter it was beyond him. He was trapped. The little fires were every-where, like green animals. Suddenly they came together in his head and he was engulfed. All he could hear was the crackle of the flames and the sound of the birds wheeling in the sky above the trees. Animal X felt himself falling. As he fell, something green and glorious inside his head pounced on him and began shaking him and filled him with pain and

'I can see perfectly well,' he repeated.

'Good,' said the longhair. 'Now: can you walk? Or will you need help with that?'

Animal X stared at her.

What followed was a series of strange and disjointed episodes. How he got from one to the next he was never entirely sure. If the fit had left him calm, it had also left him prone to sleep on his feet, with the result that as soon as he got used to being in one place, he found himself somewhere else. As soon as he became comfortable with one conversation, he seemed to be taking part in another—

The long procession, having barely reached its objective, reformed, and, with the newcomers at its head, made its way back to the village, where individual cats evaporated steadily away into their own houses and gardens until none was left. It was like seeing steam drawn back into the spout of a kettle. Animal X stopped to watch the last of them go. Night had fallen as they came up from the water-meadows: the village lay white-and-thatch under a fattening moon. There was an oak; a cenotaph; a tiny shop from which, senses sharpened by *petit mal*, he could smell oranges, liquorice, yesterday's bread. He thought he would remember it all his life – the sweet smell of bread, the cats' eyes like candles in the night, the blue-cream walking at his side like a beautiful ghost.

'Why did they come out to me?' he asked her.

'Because you are a cat. And because many of them have had experiences like yours.'

'I don't—'

'Look!' she interrupted.

Before him stood the church he had seen from the river, small, old, set amid yew-shaded graves, with a tower of soft-edged grey stone. Waiting for them in its shadowy wooden porch sat a white cat with bright blue eyes, who said, 'Well now, Amelie. What have you found for us this time?'

She was old, but her voice was firm and true. Her gaze went from Stilton to the golden kitten – on whom it rested for some time in a kind of amused maternal delight – and to ourselves. I daresay they wouldn't care that we housed you here: but what they don't know doesn't hurt them.'

'Thank you,' he said.

'No good thanking me. Can't hear a word.'

He was swaying on his feet from tiredness again. He heard her voice go away from him as she explained something to Amelie; and then Stilton saying, 'I'm Stilton, and I'm hungry.'

Then he simply fell asleep where he stood.

He woke alone, an hour or two later. Moonlight fell in a thin bar across the floor from the single window. The vestry was deserted, a little chilly. He found that he had made himself a kind of nest out of the clothes on the chair, which smelled not unpleasantly of dust and human perspiration. He felt quite hungry, though disoriented. He was getting up to go and look for his friends, and see what was happening in the village, when Amelie the blue-cream came quietly round the door, sat down beside him and began to groom herself in a self-possessed but companionable fashion. Animal X watched her for a moment or two, hypnotized by the long, soft strokes of her tongue in the cloud of bicolour fur, and rather wishing he could offer to groom her himself. Then he said, 'Why are you helping us?'

'Because you are cats.'

She seemed to consider this – as if she might qualify it in some way – but then started off in quite another direction.

'We haven't been here long ourselves,' she said. 'When we came, it was snow.' She shivered. 'It was snow everywhere. We had been taken by furriers. They stuff you in cages and drive you about for hours in a filthy vehicle, until you're sick from oil fumes and being shaken about. Horrible! It was Cottonreel who got us out of that – though she had help from a cat we never saw again – and Cottonreel who kept us together afterwards. To start with we were ordinary cats, rather out for ourselves, unable to relinquish the sheltered self-centred lives we had lost. But Cottonreel wouldn't have any of it. She is simply the most sensible animal in the world! She made sure we found homes, with humans or

She said, 'You have some way to go yet.'

'The river will bring me somewhere in the end.'

'I did not mean it in a geographical sense.' She thought for a moment. 'Though if you keep following the river it will take you to the sea. That may be no bad thing.'

'What is "the sea"?'

'Well, I will tell you, because I was once there. I caught a glimpse of it from a carrying basket, somewhere between a cat show and a car park. It was late afternoon. The air was so different! Behind me was a hall full of cats – the least of them had been judged and found acceptable. In front, a sky so bright it seemed to go on for ever!' She closed her eyes. Opened them again. 'You can see further there,' she said. 'But the sea, the sea— For one thing, it smells of salt, and cooked fish, and items which have been dead for quite a long time. For another, there are huge white birds there: birds as big as a cat, that make the loneliest noise you have ever heard. They hover for a moment, then swing away on the wind and disappear among the rooftops. The sea— The main thing to remember about the sea is that it is more water than you can ever imagine. It is so big that it heaves up and down, grey and blue, with a kind of cotton wool floating on it.' She thought for a moment. 'What else? There is always an old man leading two dogs. Oh, and at the sea, human beings walk around waving their arms and pointing things out to one another.' She cast about for one last thing to add. 'All that day I smelled fried onions,' she said. 'I was first in my class, best in show.'

When he heard about the sea, Animal X felt himself fill up like a clear glass with excitement. 'I was always going there,' he thought. He had no idea why. 'Whatever I was, I was going there.' Suddenly he thought, 'Even though I am frightened of so much water.'

To Amelie he said, 'That is where I am bound to go. That "sea".'

'Well then,' said Amelie, 'how lucky I am to have hit on it so soon. Sleep well.'

And she left him to the mirror.

*

'Ah,' said Animal X, who had suspected something like it.
'Are you sure?' he said. 'To tell you the truth, I am not
certain I remember all that. I have not had the opportunity
to do it for some time.'

She looked back down the length of her body at him.

'I will begin to think you are stupid,' she said softly.

Later, they stood side by side again, looking into the mirror,
and she told him, 'A great change is coming about in the
world. I have felt that since I was a kitten. I work here now
to help it happen; or perhaps just to be ready for it. I forget
which.'

'What was it like to be a kitten?'

'I was all success in those days,' she said.

She examined her image, next to Animal X's in the
mirror.

'But nothing lasts. We Persians find it hard to give up our
youth, especially after a career on the show bench. If we
aren't careful we become sulky, narcissistic, demanding.'

'You look beautiful to me,' said Animal X.

She rubbed her face against his.

'Oh, this body is a little too cobby now, and the fur goes
in need of a groom longer than it should—' She saw that he
was no longer listening and laughed to show she didn't
mind. 'What are you thinking?'

'There's something I have to tell you,' he said. 'We will be
the last cats who come down the river.'

'Why do you say that?'

'Something destroyed that place for good,' he said. 'Broke
it to pieces. Many of them died. We were the last to leave.'

'I don't understand.'

He said, 'Something broke it open one morning, right in
front of me, some green fire, I wasn't sure if it was there or
not. Have you ever seen anything like that?' After a
moment, when she didn't answer, he added, 'I'm sorry it
took us so long to get here. We didn't know much about
being outside.'

He said, looking in front of him, 'We'll be the last of them
now. You will need to tell the white cat that.'

remember.' It had been the Dog for a long time. 'Too long to remember how,' it concluded. 'Far too long.'

Then it thought, 'Still only one golden kitten.'

It would keep watching until dawn. It would keep watching all the next day if that proved necessary. 'A dog can watch for ever,' it thought.

It thought, 'What else is there to do?'

'It didn't come to fighting,' said Tag.

'But you were the other cat.'

'I suppose I was,' Tag said. He admitted, 'I haven't been altogether fair to you, Leonora.' He had intended to explain further, but she seemed so disheartened it made him shy. He looked away from her, and in the end all he could think of to say was, 'You don't have to be right all the time, you know. Life isn't a test.'

'Even so,' she said. 'I feel a fool.'

'You will never be a fool, Leonora,' he said as severely as he could. 'That side of things – how we are when the wild roads change us – well, it's sometimes hard for a kitten to accept. I'm the one to tell you about that: I hated those roads when I was young! They seemed so pitiless to me. You haven't quite found yourself yet, out there on the Old Changing Way. When you do, you will be something to be reckoned with. You have all your father in you, and much of your mother. You should see them when they are over there, Leo! They are the two most beautiful and terrifying animals in the world!'

She purred suddenly.

'You're my favourite animal,' she said.

'I am only Tag.'

'Tag is a lot. Tag is a very great deal.'

After this exchange both of them became thoughtful, and, in the absence of anything to say, studied the house of Uroum Bashou, the back door of which had been shoved outwards off its hinges and now leaned cheerfully awry into the garden, encouraging the sunshine to stream inside. From where he sat, Tag had an oblique view down the passageway to the bottom of the stairs. Everything in there seemed broken. The light fell on scratched paintwork, torn-up linoleum. Objects lay as if they had been thrown about – a broom-handle, a shoe ripped almost in half, a broken picture-frame. 'I warned him, I warned him,' Tag thought. 'Nothing good has gone on here.' Even the passage wain-scoting had been bruised, as if something heavy had blundered into it, cracking the tongue-and-groove boards as easily as matchsticks as it passed out of the house.

It was an effort even to look at them.

'Is it a message, Leo? Are they "words"?'

Leonora shook her head.

'I don't know,' she said.

'This was bound to happen,' said Tag sadly; then, thinking of Kater Murr, 'As for that poor, deranged animal, where will he go now? Who will look after him?'

Leo shuddered. 'No-one, I hope!' she said.

There was no point in staying. Tag let her mourn for a moment, then led her away from the Reading Cat's stiffening form. At the door she turned for one last look, as if by that she could fix the old cat in her mind for ever.

'His tail!' she cried. 'Look at his tail!'

'What?'

'The knot is gone out of it. The world has got its memory back.' She gave the wreckage a bitter look. 'I hate the way things are,' she said. 'Oh, Tag, he was so happy to be able to help me. When I last saw him here his shadow looked like ink, thrown by the moonlight on his scattered books.'

The journey to the oceanarium was silent, fraught. Since no news had arrived there of the missing tabby, Tag left Leo with her parents and took to the wild roads on his own. The news from Egypt, along with the accidental discoveries of Uroum Bashou and Leonora Whitstand Merril, had enabled him to understand several pieces of the puzzle. But they were of such strange, nightmarish shapes that they made no recognizable whole. The harder he tried to join them up, the more they resisted. How was the disease of the wild roads linked to the thing Ragnar and Pertelot had fled from in Egypt? He had a growing – and appalled – suspicion that he knew who had taken the kittens; but he had no idea how that could be, or how it fitted with the rest! Something was missing: he couldn't find it, but he couldn't stop himself from trying to fit things together without it. His worst fear was for Isis and Odin: if he was right, they were in fearful corners. Here and there a cat slept on a sofa. And from one lighted window a kitten gazed out owl-eyed and curious into the evening. He took to it for no reason he could see. It was such a nondescript little thing, saved like them all by the gawky elegance of extreme youth. Square lines, fluffy sparse fur a pale ginger colour, the tiniest paws Tag had ever seen. When he jumped onto the outside window-sill, it blinked; held its ground; then with a jerky, determined motion reared up and beat its front paws softly on the glass. In the wake of this announcement they stared at one another.

'Don't be afraid,' said Tag.

The kitten fluffed itself up.

'Why would I be?' it said. 'I'm bigger than you.'

'I didn't notice that at first.'

'This light is poor,' the kitten acknowledged comfortably.

After a moment, he wasn't sure why, Tag said, 'When I was about your age I was taken away on a great adventure. I lost my home and my life was changed for ever. Was it a good thing or a bad thing? I still don't know.'

'I would like to go on an adventure,' said the kitten wistfully. 'Have you come to fetch me?'

'Certainly not!' said Tag.

He was horrified. 'Stay at home,' he advised. 'What are your owners like?'

'Dull. Nice, but dull.'

'Ah.'

There was a pause.

'I expect they give you pretty good stuff to eat, though,' Tag said. 'Game casserole, meat-and-liver dinner, fishes in tins, all that sort of thing?'

The kitten examined him.

'Anyone can get that,' it said.

Tag, who had experienced such confidence himself, felt there was a further argument to be made. Somehow, though, it escaped him. 'Well, anyway,' he said. 'You want to stay in, where it's safe.' He jumped down off the window-sill. 'Another thing, never pay any attention to what a bird says.' Suddenly unsure of what he had achieved here, and looking for some final expression of a position fatally un-the battle at Tintagel, he had travelled across the country with Francine and, for a while, Sealink. How Sealink and Francine had bickered and fought. The discovery of the dead badger. Francine's tumble into the rabbit trap, and the consequences of that. It was a long story and finally a sad one, a story of hard travel, mismatched companions, happiness fading to puzzlement.

'When we set out,' he said, 'we were so hopeful. The Alchemist was defeated. We had our lives to live.' He stared across the lawn. 'Then Sealink and Francine began scratching away at one another like that. I knew they didn't get on, of course. I knew that from the start. But I thought—' He shook his head sadly. 'I don't know what I thought. My life had been given back to me in more ways than one. If I was free of the Alchemist, I was free of Majicou too. I was changed, and I expected everyone else to be. There was such a spirit of generosity on that headland after we won the battle. And yet within days those two had frittered it away! I couldn't blame either of them. That calico cat, she's in full sail the moment she wakes up – she never gives an inch. She'd lost her mate and she isn't good at loss. She was full of guilt – even as she left us, she was transferring it to some obsession with kittens she had abandoned long ago. I wonder where she is now? She's a tough old thing, but she can't bring back the past any more than you can.' There was a silence. Then he shrugged. 'As for Francine, well, Francine had her faults. I'd be the first to admit it. Her world was narrow, she never understood the events that caught her up. She was just a fox. But Tag, I never saw a fox so beautiful as her!'

He fell silent and stared at the floor.

'What happened?' Tag asked him.

No answer.

'We can't help who we love,' said Tag. This made him think suddenly of Cy, off somewhere in the deep world without him. He surprised himself further by adding, 'Love lies in wait and forces us to care.'

The fox gave Tag an anguished look, then stared hard into the dark as if the past still lay there, just out of sight.

of the lawn. There he got up awkwardly on his hind legs, and, with his front paws resting either side of the water, drank from it, lapping noisily for what seemed like some minutes. When he had finished he dropped onto all fours again and walked stiffly to the far edge of the lawn.

'Are you going?' said Tag. 'Don't you want to hear what happened to me?'

The fox looked back at him.

'I am trying to work the arthritis out of my leg,' he said. 'Ah.'

'So then tell me.'

Tag began by describing the oceanarium, and how he had lived there with Cy and been happier than at any other time in his life. He touched briefly on the domestic arrangements of the King and Queen. How they too had prospered. From there he moved on to the inexplicable loss of Odin and Isis. He drew the fox's attention to the mysteries attendant on this: the signs and symbols he could not interpret; the journeys which seemed to fold into themselves and reveal nothing; the proxies who brought back no answers. He spoke of the hard death of Uroum Bashou. 'Something is wrong in the world,' he said, 'and I am followed everywhere I go. I fear the worst. Who does the Great Ray serve, and why did it take the Mau to Egypt? Where is Cy? What is happening along the wild roads?' He sighed exasperatedly. 'The clues mean nothing to me, and I am in a fog,' he concluded. Then he sat back and waited for the fox's opinion.

But Loves A Dustbin only said, 'It was clever to take the third kitten as your apprentice. The Old Majicou would have appreciated that.'

'I feel the weight of these responsibilities,' Tag prompted. 'I don't know what to do.'

The fox greeted this admission in silence, its eyes yellow with some emotion Tag couldn't interpret. Then it ordered, 'Come with me,' and, plunging immediately through the overgrown hedge, set off across the gardens at a pace Tag soon found difficult to maintain. They squeezed between the loose boards of fences. They trotted down the passageways

'I would act if I knew how.'

'"If I knew how"!' mimicked the fox. 'You hoped Uroum Bashou would tell you what to do. You hoped I would.' He stared contemptuously up at the lighted house. 'And what can you learn here, sniffing around after your kittenhood?' He sighed. 'You are the New Majicou,' he said heavily, 'like it or not. I can serve you as well as I served the old one: but you must make yourself worth the effort. Everyone depends on you.' There was a long pause, in which the two animals stood looking defiantly at one another. In the end, Tag blurted out the thing that worried him most, the thing he had been trying to keep from himself:

'The Alchemist is still alive.'

It was a relief to have it in the open.

'We didn't save the world back then,' he said. 'We only thought we did.'

The fox stared at him.

'Then what are you going to do?' he demanded. 'Francine and One For Sorrow and all the others: are they going to have died for nothing?'

'I would not allow that,' said Tag, holding the fox's eye with his own. 'Did you imagine I would?'

The fox looked away.

'Of course not,' he said.

'Then let's not quarrel any more. I must speak with Ragnar Gustaffson. We may not be too late if we act now. One avenue remains, and I will need his support, as well as yours, if I am to explore it.'

'That's more like it!' applauded Loves A Dustbin. 'Good!'

Tag laughed. His spirits lifted. Friendship had returned to him the energy leached out by frustration. He felt like a giant. He remembered the fox, long ago, dancing round a lamppost in winter light and sleet. He remembered a black and white bird, so full of itself it fell off a post.

'Creatures of Majicou!' he whispered to himself.

'Pardon?'

'I said, "We must be quick."'

'Then it's the mirror for us!' cried the fox, and sprang towards the back of the arbour. With a feral grin and a

XV

A Message

'Well, that got me a whole load of nowhere,' the calico grumbled bitterly.

The Mammy's pronouncements had left her feeling quite defeated. Tough-spirited and enterprising, Sealink would never normally have given herself up to self-pity, but now, surrounded by hostile swamps, in a country she no longer recognized as home, having travelled perilously to seek the answer to a problem not of her own making, and that 'answer' having proved utterly impenetrable, she found her usual optimism slipping like a spider down a plughole. Everything was so much larger and more complicated than she had ever expected. She saw herself suddenly, with unprecedented objectivity, as a tiny mote of life spinning, lonely and desolate, in a void.

'You lost, ma'am?'

Alerted as much by a strange, musky scent as by the question, Sealink's head shot up. Staring inquisitively at her was the second of the guards she had encountered earlier at the bone-pile. She recovered her composure with impressive speed.

'I guess so. Lost in all senses of the word.'

The guard made a sort of hoarse snuffle. 'The Mammy has that kind of effect on folks. Bet you're no nearer knowing what to do than you were when you came here, huh?'

Sealink shook her head. 'Whole loada stuff she sang out. Can't recall more'n a few words here an' there, and they're not all that *indicative*, y'know? Don't help none that a lot of it was foreign.'

The guard made a stiff little bow. 'Allow me, ma'am, to

239

She'd known a few black cats in her life. Cyrus and William; Earwax and Amphetamine . . . These were all at once obliterated by the vision of a black cat's head, flayed and displayed in a voodoo-shop window . . .

'The Baron,' she breathed.

The armadillo considered Sealink neutrally. 'If that means something to you, sister, then that's fine by me. He likely to eat the world?'

Sealink stared at him.

'*Mange le monde.* Or maybe even *mangent le monde.* Might be more than one of 'em.'

The calico shrugged. 'He had a good life in his time, the Baron, but he weren't ever ill-intentioned. Loved life. I guess you could say he wanted to "eat the world". But he was alone when last I saw him.' She shivered. 'Beyond that I don't got the least idea.' She wrinkled her brow and thought about the rest of the Mammy's divinations. '*Rues sauvages*, moo— something; and a pyramid, *cassé*, and,' she concentrated hard, '*les trois sont perdus.*'

'Wild roads. Moo— MOO!' A bellow that made Sealink jump. 'Ain't too many cattle round here!' He cackled, Mammy-like. The calico fixed him with such a fierce glare that he felt compelled to drop his gaze and scratch nervously at his neck. He dug around for a moment in the vulnerable area where two armoured plates met, then examined his nails and sucked out the fruits of their labour. Head on one side, he considered the possibilities. 'Moo— moolah: money. No. Can't be. *Mourir* – to die, maybe. The wild roads are dying.'

Sealink nodded slowly.

'Sounds ominous.' He steepled his fingers, then moved his hands apart. 'Onward, onward. Pyramid *cassé* . . . *trois sont perdus* . . . hmm . . . Broken pyramid; and three are lost. Three. Prime number, very powerful: lots of magical things come in threes. Three wishes; three questions. Three wise men. The three holy threads of the ancient Brahmin. The Three Graces. The Three Fates. The Holy Trinity. According to Pythagoras the perfect number. But the three are lost? You got me there.'

been, Clete . . . Taller'n we ever . . . managed before . . . Y'all said . . . the triangle was the strongest . . . engineering . . . structure in the world . . . and I know I ain't always . . . too bright, but I guess it . . . filtered through in the end . . . kinda came to me . . . in a flash—'

This exposition came to an unceremonious halt as Cletus stopped in his tracks and his companion cannoned into him.

In the middle of the glade the bone-pile towered, its lines cleanly and improbably geometrical, the harsh noon light transforming the white of the skeletal remains to a gold so bright it hurt the eyes.

Sealink stared at it and felt distant echoes stir inside her head.

A tall triangle – a pyramid – and, balanced impossibly upon its apex, making all perspectives unreliable, the Louisiana sun, blazing like a message from the entire natural world.

That night, far from the Mammy and her armadillos, far from alligators and dragonflies that talked; far from the vision of a bone-pile gleaming like a neon message, the calico cat slept, exhausted by her long trek.

And, as she slept, she was visited by a dream.

As dreams go, it was neither particularly horrifying, nor did it hold the sweet sensuality of the golden reveries she had experienced in her youth. Despite this, when she awoke, she found that she was shaking; but whether this reaction sprang from fear or a sudden and inexplicable optimism, or maybe from some adrenalizing combination of the two, she could not say.

As the sun rose over the distant horizon, so did Sealink. Tail up, chin high, the calico strode purposefully down the dirt road which she knew, as cats do from their deep internal navigations, would eventually lead back to the city of her birth.

She was Sealink, and she had a job to do.

What had followed, she claimed, wasn't so easy to understand –

As soon as the King and Queen were safely disembarked,
the Great Ray had furled and folded himself and whirled
down into the tank again, back onto the Fish Road. 'There
was no time for me to get off! I was stuck! Tag, I was so
excited! He was saying things to me. We were going on the
journey of a lifetime, me and that fish. That was what he
promised, and it was true. Soon we're down in the deeps of
the sea, which is like some electric church where the inhabitants got their own light. Tag, these are guys that glow in
the dark!'

South went the great fish, then east and west. Each time
he surfaced it was to show her something new about the
world. Humid green jungles that came down to the water,
releasing flocks of birds like coloured laundry. An island no
more than a smoking cone, hot cinders in the air ten miles
out to sea, smells that made her nose run. 'I seen the bows
of broken ships, ghostly in pale sea-bottom mud, all them
long-ago captains fishbait now! And a beach where striped
cats came down to swim in the huge waves – I would've
liked to join them, but of course,' she said with a certain
regret, 'they were bigger than me.' Shores like deserts,
shores like jewels, shores blackened with oil and scattered
with towers and huge machines. 'Oh I felt sad, Tag, some of
those things I seen!'

At last the ray turned north; and from the deepest journey
of all they surfaced in a strip of benighted water like black
glass. There was snow and ice as far as the eye could see.
Huge pieces of this frozen landscape toppled into the sea
around her while she watched. 'It was hurling itself in, that
stuff. It was the biggest *sugar* I ever saw. I say to Ray, "This
stuff is whiter than you!" He says nothing. I thought he was
nervous, you know? But it wasn't that. He was just getting
ready.' Plumes of water rose in slow motion as the ice cliffs
fell, only to subside in total silence as if she were watching
through a sheet of glass. 'Tag, even my eyes were cold. Brrr!'
All the while, her friend lay on the water, slowly revolving,
like a compass needle, until, in the sky, she saw the aurora,

no cats nor human beings nor nothing.'

She shivered.

'So we came back, as quick as we could. Oh, Ray wanted to go on somewhere else, but I said, "Take me home." I'm keen on Ray, but sometimes it's hard to get him to stop. That fish has got a real urge to see things. I asked him how this Road of his goes so many places, even the Moon, which he had to admit he didn't like either. He told me, "Little Warm Sister – " because he calls me that, his Little Warm Sister " – the fishes were here before anyone else. We grew restless, and swam down to Earth before anyone else arrived.'

She was silent for a moment.

'Does that make any sense to you?' she said.

Tag said nothing. He couldn't think.

Then she jumped to her feet. 'Look! Tag! The boats. The boats!' And there they were, the fishing-boats returning safe home, a line of lights bobbing at the harbour mouth. And, behind them, the first green flare of the dawn. Cy broke into a great, clattering purr.

Tag felt himself fill with love.

'I'm glad you're back,' he said. 'I missed you.'

On the way back up to the oceanarium, she tried to explain how she had felt when she fell in the tank. 'At first,' she said, 'I thought I'd had it. I thought I was going dancing with Davy Jones.' But, even as she touched the water, she had felt supported, in a way she couldn't now explain. 'Ray wasn't there then,' she said. 'It was as if something else held me up. Tag, it was like warm green hands in the water!'

Then she asked, 'Why does a fish make friends with a cat?'

'I think that's what I was asking you,' said Tag.

Cy looked up at him uncertainly.

'I wonder what the end of all this will be,' she said.

Tag looked down at the harbour, and the gulls wheeling round the fishing-boats; then up at the oceanarium, where they would be waiting for the New Majicou to make decisions.

'Yes.'

Leonora herself broke this deadlock. 'Where is it you want to go?' she asked Tag.

'Be quiet, Leonora!' ordered the Mau.

'This is my life too you know,' said Leonora.

'Leonora!'

'What if Odin and Isis are there?'

'What if they aren't?' said the Mau tiredly. 'Am I to lose you, too?'

'If we falter now—' Tag began.

' – we may lose everything,' finished the Queen. 'I have heard that argument before.'

But Leonora said, 'I am not a kitten any more. I want my brother and sister back, and I want to play my part.'

'Then play it,' said Pertelot.

And she turned her back.

'Where do you want to go?' Leonora asked Tag.

'For hundreds of years the Alchemist had a house outside the city. I found it after I became the Majicou. I go there now and then—'

' – in case he comes back!'

'I don't know. Perhaps. I go there as I go to the pet shop in Cutting Lane. The Majicou is a caretaker, but to an extent he must intuit his own duties. I followed my nose, and the wild roads showed me that house. Ever since, though I hate the place, it has seemed to me to be part of my domain. I was there the day your brother vanished.'

Tag shook his head.

'We might find answers there,' he went on. 'But the danger is obvious.'

Leonora absorbed this in a kind of awed silence.

Then she said, 'Wow! The Alchemist! What do you want me to do?'

The Mau laughed angrily.

'Oh, you learned plenty from your predecessor,' she congratulated Tag. 'That one-eyed cat always knew the right thing to say.'

The gardens had deteriorated since Tag's last visit. The

built a fire in the middle of the marble floor, using lumber from the adjoining rooms. Around its ashes were scattered empty gas cylinders, fast-food trays, the rags of blankets. 'Human beings have been living here,' decided Tag, wrinkling his nose at the sad odours of charred wood, stale food, urine.

The fox looked up.

'If you had a sense of smell,' he said, 'you would know more than that.'

He had been sniffing intently about at the bottom of the stairs. Now he trotted across the room and gazed out over the lawns. 'And yet I didn't notice it out there,' he told himself thoughtfully.

'Didn't notice what?' said Tag.

'That's the thing,' said Loves A Dustbin. 'I don't know. Something else has been here recently. It wasn't human, but it certainly wasn't a cat.'

'Where is Leonora?' said Ragnar.

Growing bored with their investigations, his daughter had taken to the stairs: by the time they thought to look for her, she was already two or three floors up.

There, gilt and marble gave way to fumed-oak panelling. The landings were narrower, the windows smaller and less well-proportioned. Cobwebs stretched in tight curves, dusty muslin set across every corner as if to trap the twilight. Underfoot was a gritty loess compounded of house-dust, fallen plaster, ash and soot expelled from ancient hearths. Small cold draughts crept forth to brush away Leonora's footprints as she passed. The stairwell closed in above her. She stopped in a ray of light from the last west-facing window – looked up, one paw raised – ran on. It was almost dark when she reached the room below the copper dome, and found its door jammed open.

'I didn't feel frightened,' she would insist later. 'Not frightened, not at first.'

It was a tall room with a ceiling shaped like an inverted tulip, braced by a tangle of old wooden beams. The walls had once been distempered white. Along them ran scarred led in disarray, their covers stripped, their pages like broken white wings in the gathering darkness. It was the books which brought him to a halt.

'Look at this, Leo,' he said.

He said, 'My pride is to blame for this.'

He laughed.

'What we have just seen here was a sideshow,' he told himself. 'Not the main event. I saw that plainly, yet—'

His tail lashed from side to side.

'I have been a complete fool!' he cried.

'Ragnar! Loves A Dustbin! Think back,' he asked them, 'to the battle with the Alchemist. We were scattered in disarray across Tintagel Head. He loomed above us like death. Everything was lost, until the birth of the kittens! The Alchemist stared down at them, cried out something like dismay, and faltered. In that moment, we had him. But we never asked ourselves why! We never asked what he had seen, what he had guessed, or why he lost his nerve so completely.

'Once I had recognized and accepted what happened in that moment,' he told them, 'so much of what has been hidden was made clear to me! There was no Golden Cat in the Mau's litter – only three odd but delightful kittens, each with a clear and recognizable quality of its own. We have asked ourselves again and again which of them might wear the mantle – Leo the dancer, full of subtlety and life; Isis the singer, whose voice speaks to the unseen, the way between the worlds; Odin the hunter, closer of the circle. None of them has yet turned out to be what the Alchemist was seeking – the magic animal whose creation he had worked towards for three hundred years –'

'Yet the Golden Cat has been with us since the moment Pertelot gave birth.

'Oh, it is a paradox, I admit, but I should have resolved it sooner. It is a tangled skein, but that is no excuse. Still – ' here he stared grimly round. ' – I am the Majicou, and I believe we are still in time to retrieve the situation. Leo, stay close: without you they can do nothing. Hurry! We must get back to the oceanarium!'

interpret the fresh scuff-marks on the tiled floor.

Leonora had almost reached the door when the air in the centre of the room began to fluoresce faintly. A few whitish sparks formed about a foot above the floor and drifted to and fro, first attracted to then repulsed by a strange, smoky twist of light. The light was breathing. Leonora could hear it. Sparks went in and out. Then, after a moment or two, a small convulsion like a sneeze took place, and a current of warm air was expelled into the room. Sparks whirled up now, as if from a bonfire. She heard faint music. There was a popping sound, an apologetic cough. Leonora could not move. There was a flaw in the solid world, a discontinuity which grew and grew, then parted like rubbery human lips in the fabric of that nightmare place, onto a darkness which curdled and took shape before her –

Ragnar Gustaffson and Loves A Dustbin reached the top of the house just in time to hear Leonora's shriek of anger. When they burst into the room beneath the dome, it was full of brown shadows, disconnected movements, something that looked like smoke. Ragnar Gustaffson stood there confusedly for a moment, his eyes watering in the chemical reek, convinced the house was on fire.

'Leonora!' he called.

'I can't see her!' yelped the fox. 'I can't see her!'

'Leonora!' they called together. 'Leonora!'

But the New Majicou, arriving a little later, and entering the room with a curious mixture of calm and reluctance, narrowed his eyes and said nothing at all.

Leonora had backed deep into the gap between two wooden cupboards, and now – wedged fast, bubbling and spitting as much with loss of dignity as fear – faced the danger with bared claws. Above her, pacing angrily to and fro like a tiger in a cage, loomed a thing half cat, half man, the two halves shifting and roiling one into the other, one moment joined, the next separate, never quite properly connected, like shapes in a dream. It was bigger than any real human being. It was there, but it wasn't there. It was

Racing to keep up, his friends followed him back down the stairs, across the sodden lawn and into the highway by the boat-house.

PART THREE

The Bright Tapestry

XVII

The Fields of the Blessed

So it was with all the brazen opportunism of her earlier life that much later that day Sealink strolled up to a busy bait-shop in the middle of a small fishing-town and listened intently to a group of men leaning against a dusty pick-up, drinking beer as the sun went down. When the group split and two of them climbed into the truck and pulled away, bound with their haul of crawfish for the Friday market, they left with an extra load on board: a thirteen-pound calico cat, already intent on making herself at least a fourteen-pound cat by the time they arrived at their mutual destination, by availing herself of their abundant hospitality . . .

In the dream it had seemed both extraordinary and perfectly normal that the Majicou, that mystical guardian of the roads, should appear to her and speak warmly, as to a life-long friend. When first he had shown her his face it was in his guise as old black tomcat, a little greyed and ragged, his single pale eye stern yet gleaming with vitality. Yet it was in this embodiment that she found him most awesome, for she could sense that this manifestation was in some way a display, most likely directed not at her, of his burning will and self-determination – a measure of his true power.

'I apologize,' the Majicou said. 'My experiment with the Mammy and her bones was not entirely successful. I must, it seems, try something more straightforward. I can only pray I am granted the time . . .

'Come with me, Sealink, trust me – '

The next moment, the black cat was gone, and Sealink found herself slipping deeper in the dream, into a more profound and wilder place by far.

something Sealink was used to. It made her head hurt. And, the more her head ached, the more elusive the symbol became.

All at once there was a roar in the darkness, and the golden triangle broke apart into its component lines, shivering in the air. One aspect of it spiralled deliberately in front of her for a moment, then it was gone; only to be replaced a second later by a small shape, a tiny golden creature which stared helplessly upward as if beset by something dark and formless, something which leaned over it in predatory rapture.

Sealink felt her heart thump painfully.

It was a kitten . . .

At once a great wave of empathy and love flowed out from her towards this helpless creature. Something in her recognized it, not only as a kitten in distress, but as a kitten she *knew*. Somehow – she could not imagine how, or why – one of Pertelot's beloved kittens was in danger. She felt its presence, reaching out for her, and she felt, like a red blast in her head, its fury and its pain. The vision dissolved into night. This was followed by a flash, almost subliminal, of a city skyline, a city she knew well – then all was dark again.

Oblivious to fear in the heart of the dream, Sealink embraced her fate.

'Majicou, help me to find this kitten!'

Silence. Silence and darkness. A rush of air.

Then she was back in the presence of the great cat. The tobacco-brown rosettes shifted and flowed beneath the oily sheen of his fur. He opened his mouth and roared, 'There are miracles in this life, as there are in all lives. Take on this task and save the Golden Cat. Wish for the most impossible thing in the world with the wildest part of yourself and it shall be yours.' He cocked his head. The one eye shone like a lamp. 'Go now, Sealink, I—'

Suddenly he began to dwindle, his mouth opening and closing silently; then he started to spin away as if caught in the vortex of terrible power.

A wild thought struck the tigress, as if from another life. 'The Fields of the Blessed!' she called after his receding form. 'Where can I find them?'

'*Move, and the world moves with you.*' So she had advised the Queen of Cats on the deck of a bobbing boat that was bearing them away from a city filled with horrors, a city on another continent entirely. '*That's what travelling's for – putting distance between yourself and your past.*'

And yet here she was: travelling straight back into the arms of her own.

Strangely enough, it felt right. Straightforward to the point of bluntness, Sealink was inclined to tackle matters head-on. She greatly preferred administering a sharp cuff upside the ear to the use of tact. And she was looking forward to applying a bit of that specialism to an old friend.

She had already marked Kiki La Doucette down as her first objective.

Sealink stored up her grudges with fastidious care, keeping them safely parcelled away in a quiet place in her head, only to be taken out and dealt with when the right opportunity presented itself. And some grudges were more significant than others.

She could understand why Kiki might want to surround herself with sycophantic hangers-on who brought her so much food she became gargantuan. Hell: yes. She could understand that.

Old insults and scratches traded down on the boardwalk when the Delta Queen had been coming into her sexual maturity; lovers lost and lovers stolen: nothing so terrible there.

But Kiki was a stealer of kittens.

She had stolen the kittens of the cemetery cats.

And she had stolen Sealink's own. The calico considered for a brief moment how Kiki had, in fact, rescued the survivors, then dismissed the thought entirely. What remained was that she had left two to gasp out their last breaths on the river's cold shoreline. She had raised another two in her own vile image. And she knew the whereabouts of the fifth.

Find her, then, and settle the score. If anyone knew the whereabouts of kittens, it was Kiki La Doucette.

*

But it was less the ashes than their provenance that held Sealink in thrall: for, bound to the grate with wire, its whole body twisted up and away from where the flames must have leapt, was a skeletal shape, all clumped and charred like ancient, flaky wrought iron, the tragic remnants of its head a rictus of silent agony and outrage. In the midst of so much soot, its teeth shone white as pearls, weaponry terribly outclassed by that of its opponents.

Sealink felt her legs go from under her. She sat down on the cold, hard stone and felt shocked reaction shudder through her in waves.

Someone had burned a cat. Deliberately, and in a very public place.

Without any conscious thought, she found her feet and put them to good use. She ran and ran through the dawn-lit streets until stopped by the four-lane highway of North Rampart. On the other side of the road, the crumbling walls of the old boneyard rose up; above them, still white angels and a woman with a cross, her hand raised in greeting, or warning. Early-morning traffic rumbled past, expelling noxious fumes. Sealink breathed deeply. Even diesel oil was preferable to the stench that followed her, so she sat by the side of the road and let the exhaust smoke infuse her coat.

She sat there, motionless, in a sort of daze.

The next thing she knew, there was a screech of brakes and a shrill voice shrieking out of a car window, 'Look – a great big one – we could get at least ten dollars for it!'

There was a din of doors opening and slamming and a clamour of voices, and Sealink ran for her life. A big ten-wheeler missed her by inches, its airhorn blaring wildly. A station-wagon swerved around her; in the other direction, a truck jammed on its brakes and its tyres screeched against the tarmac. The last car came straight at her. She just had time to see a pair of hands clutching the steering-wheel with white knuckles, a manic face leaning forward, mouth open in fury or triumph, and then there was darkness. Hot metal seared the fur on her back. A fiery pain and burning fur. Vile fumes engulfed her. Sealink had time to feel a terrible, sad irony at this useless loss of life, then suddenly there was light

They laughed at us – too sick, too tired and slow to stop 'em.' He sighed.

'We've had a few new arrivals since then. Owners kicked 'em out, decided they didn't like cats after all. Now we're all starvin' together—'

He stopped abruptly, for he had lost the calico's attention. She was staring above his head, eyes round with surprise. Her whiskers trembled. Then her coral lips stretched into the most beatific of smiles.

'My, my – fallen on hard times, have you, my angels? Seems there may be a little justice in the world after all.'

Crouched on top of the tomb above Hog, under the protective hands of a praying plaster child, were two large tabby cats, their coats a little thinner, their expressions a little less assured, their mannerisms a little less arrogant than the last time Sealink had seen them, in the dusty storeroom of the Golden Scarab bookshop.

Kiki's helpers.

Venus and Sappho.

Sealink's daughters.

And even as she recognized them she remembered something else, something that had evaded her all this time.

Life had recently dealt the erstwhile bookshop cats a number of setbacks; but the revelation of one half of their parentage left them speechless with disbelief. Sealink watched with slow, grim satisfaction as the information settled and was absorbed.

'Well, I guess you never could accuse Kiki of behaving towards us in a motherly way,' Sappho said eventually. 'She'd upped and gone by the time we were thrown out. Didn't leave any forwarding address.'

'She can't have gone far, not being so fat'n'all,' said Hog. 'But no-one's seen her around in the last day or so.'

'Not since the burning.' Venus hung her head.

Sealink turned upon her. 'What do you know about that?'

'I heard it was a cat who crossed her was burned.'

The calico shook her head slowly. 'None of this makes sense to me. Whole world's gone crazy. Sure wasn't Kiki

'What?' cried Venus impatiently. 'What then?'

Celeste scratched her ear. 'I ain't sure if I should tell you this next bit or not. Y'all t'ink I gone nuts.'

'We won't, I promise,' Hog said gently. He held the colourpoint's amber gaze for a moment or two till she carried on.

'*Eh bien* – Now of all my faculties, it's my hearin' bin least affected, so y'all got no cause to t'ink I gone deaf or crazy, y'hear? On all that's sacred, I heard it sigh, and then all those flies they spoke wit' a man's voice.'

Sealink frowned. 'Honey, run that past me again?'

'I know flies don't usually talk – '

Sealink squinted at her.

' – but I know what I heard. The wind, it sighed and it buzzed, and then it spoke with a human's voice, and it said, quite clearly: *Come here, my dear: I need your soul, too.* And then there's this other voice, deep and dark, like it's tryin' to drown out the first one. A cat's voice. So *then* I lissen real good: and it sayin', over and over: *Save the kittens. For the sake of all cats, save the kittens* . . . And then there's a great roar from inside the wind, and then, well then, *chers*, then I took off as fast as my old legs'd carry me, and even so, I swear I could hear the buzzin' of those flies and Madam Kiki laughin' at me all the way.

'There's witchery abroad, *mes chers*, witchery and mayhem.'

Later that night the boneyard cats sat huddled together inside one of the larger tombs. There was nothing left to eat. Sealink had searched the garbage cans in the nearby projects and come away empty-pawed. She had, in fact, discovered the remains of some spicy chicken in one plastic sack and without a second's pause had wolfed it down, and only then found herself trembling with embarrassment at her own greed; but the shame barely outlasted the taste of the spices.

In order to assuage her conscience she went out to look for more, and discovered her luck had not, after all, deserted her. Some kids, returning with take-out from a local Chinese, were fooling around on their bikes. Remembering

There was a sharp intake of breath. Venus stared at her mother, aghast.

'Kiki's *cadeau*.' It was less a question than a statement of fact.

'Kiki's *cadeau*. The package you two offered up to me. The one I dragged through the streets of the Quarter. The one Red tried to persuade me to open. And I, stupid and uncomprehending, refused to do so; gave him a darned good bite for his pains and hurried off to present it to Madame Kiki nice and intact. And when I laid it down on the ground at her feet, it squirmed, right there in front of me! And what did I do?' She laughed bitterly. 'I ran away. It's something I've become damn good at lately.'

'We didn't know it was a kitten.' Even Sappho, the snootier of the two, looked shocked. She stared at her sister. 'We wouldn't have given her a *kitten*. Let alone a *golden* kitten . . .'

'A golden kitten is sacred to the Great Cat . . .'

'It is a powerful being . . .'

'Enough of the metaphysics,' Sealink said briskly. 'All I know is I got a job to do, and it starts with Kiki La Doucette. I met up with her mother in the bayous—'

'Eponine Lafeet!' Celeste's tail twitched rapidly.

Hog looked surprised.

'Kiki's the Mammy's *daughter*?'

'*Chéri*, you just too young to remember,' admonished the colourpoint.

'Honey,' Sealink addressed herself to the big stripy cat. 'Don't you go strainin' your brain none.' She raised her voice. 'Yep. The Mammy. She said to me, amongst a load of nonsense I can't understand, something about seeking a sun of fire in the Fields of the Blessed. Now I don't know what the hell that means, but it seems to me that if Kiki ain't in any of her normal haunts, these fields is where I might find her.'

Sappho laughed. 'Paradise? Kiki La Doucette in the Happy Land?'

Sealink looked puzzled. 'Ain't that a bar down on Bourbon –'

'What you want with *dat* old bag of bones?'

The calico persisted. 'Do you know where I might find her?'

'Sure, if you wants a ride in a cart that overturns. Maybe get kicked in the stomach if you're real lucky. Besides, what's a cat doin' out on the streets of this city, as bold as a mutt?'

Sealink didn't feel all that bold at the moment.

'Don't you know there's a price on your head?' the mule continued mercilessly. 'If Shine don't get you then the Pestmen will!' It whinnied its amusement. 'Humans, they don't like cats none at the present time. Burned one down near the Cabildo yesterday. Boy, did that smell *bad*.'

'Look. I'm risking my neck here. Do you know where Shine is or not?'

No reply.

'Or the Elysian Fields?'

The mule bent its head round and gave her a hard look.

'I ain't speaking to *you* of such things. You's a *cat*.' In case Sealink hadn't noticed. 'But if you want Shine you might go right the way back down Decatur, by the market, where you'll find a café servin' Creole food. Can't recall the name, but you'll have no problem findin' it. Its window gets all steamed up. That's where Joe goes when trade's bad, parks the cart right outside. Old Shine, she give us all a bad name, so we don't make room for her in the queue. I hear old Joe's going to retire her soon. Won't be before time. No, ma'am.'

Sealink didn't even hear this last remark: she was already haring up the street to her companions.

In the shadow of the parked car, they stared out at her, round-eyed.

'Did you find her?' Hog asked.

'Follow me.'

Past the Margaritaville and on towards the crossroad with Barracks, the north end of Decatur street was a quiet and seedy place at this time of night. This suited Sealink's purpose fine, since, where it was darker, there were

The mule dipped its head conspiratorially. 'Want to go for a ride?'

'What?'

'Come for a ride – you and your friends. I ain't tied up.'

Sealink hesitated, then she grinned. 'Hell, why not? We got nothing to lose.'

And so it was that some minutes later a small black gig with a fringed canopy and wheels gaily painted in red might have been seen disappearing smartly up Esplanade, heading lakeside with a crew of five cats. As they went, the calico sat on the mule's back, her claws buried anxiously in the leather harness, and explained their situation to Shine: how a cat called Kiki La Doucette had betrayed her own kind; how people were paying for cats to be caught and killed; how they had burned a cat at Jackson Square; and how a very special kitten – and a great deal more – was at risk.

Shine was philosophical. 'Man is a fierce wild animal at heart,' she opined. 'We usually see him only in that tamed condition of restraint known as civilization, and so,' she turned her head in order to make eye contact with the cat on her shoulder, 'the occasional outbreaks of its true nature terrify us.'

Some time later they crossed a turning bounded by clapboard houses with peeling blue shutters and came upon a yellow dog sitting by the side of the road. It had no collar and its tongue lolled cheerfully out of its mouth. As they approached it looked up and did a double take. Its lower jaw hung suddenly slack.

'Hi there, honey!' Sealink declared cheerfully.

The dog gazed at her. 'Oh my Lord,' it said. 'Do I truly see a mule-cart full of cats driving up Esplanade?'

'You sure do, son.' Sealink was enjoying herself.

The dog started to trot alongside. 'May I be so bold,' it said, keeping pace with Shine, claws tapping on the sidewalk, 'as to enquire why that might be?'

The calico laughed, a little bitterly. 'Honey, it's a nice night.'

The dog cocked its head at her. The moonlight glinted off

and at last came to rest in a heap amongst a clutter of terra-cotta and pelargoniums.

With the adrenalin of outrage combating any immediate sense of physical injury, she sat up and looked around. It would be hard to pretend that ploughing through a hedge had been deliberate. Had anyone seen her ignominious descent? The yellow dog was still at the junction, his sharp muzzle turned in her direction. Sealink ducked away from his steady gaze and started to groom furiously, noticing as she did so that her head hurt and one eye was already begin-ning to close.

'Hell of a day,' she muttered.

Satisfied with the cursory licking, she shook out each leg in turn and a shower of privet twigs, dirt and geranium petals scattered from the long Maine Coon coat. Everything appeared to be in working order. Sealink nodded grimly, then clenched her teeth and leapt the fence to follow the disappearing buggy.

The yellow dog watched all this with a quizzical expression on his face. This was a crazy place. Still, that big old calico cat sure had some grit. Grinning lopsidedly he followed the strange cavalcade as it rounded the bend into the long, wide, nondescript boulevard known as the Elysian Fields.

'Work: The Great Liberator' read the proclamation in rusted wrought iron on either side of the black-barred gates. Raised after the fire that swept the city in 1794, on the Feast of the Immaculate Conception, the building behind these gates had been in its time a mill and a cotton warehouse, stuffed with bales for export to the Old World; a slave market, a poorhouse and latterly the place where the broken-down working horses and mules of the city were sent to be despatched into the great blue beyond; or, more likely, into a thousand cans of dogfood. Down the genera-tions, borrowing from the road on which it resided some of the sense of the original Greek, it had passed into mythology as a place of well-earned peace: the fields of the blessed.

It had not operated as a knacker's yard for some time now.

Pageant Stair, a warehouse that stank of terror and human sweat, smoke and friar's balsam; where a defiant queen and her brave king had faced off the Alchemist and an army of cats with eyes as empty as glass.

She stared. There was smoke here, too: a lot of smoke. Some came from exotic incense and vast candles burning in brass dishes; but the stuff that stung her eyes came from the pyre that dominated the centre of the great stone floor. As the smoke eddied and whirled, Sealink could make out a pile of bones, higher and more newly rendered than the last she had seen, a great heap of skeletal remains spitting out flame and reeking vapour.

A bonfire.

A sun of fire.

A bone-fire.

On the top its latest victim, unrecognizable in its death-throes, rested on a dozen others whose fur still smouldered and whose glazed eyes reflected ever more dimly the leaping flames. All around moved humans in dark robes.

As the mule-cart gatecrashed into their gathering, these humans stared at the intruders, mouths open, almost comic in their surprise. Some held cats by the scruff of the neck, bodies drooping, all the fight gone out of them. Others dragged crates closer to the pyre, fiddled with hinges, clumsy in their big leather gloves. Others still poked at the fire, feeding it with a fuel that sent up unnatural-looking flames of green and blue. A smaller group knelt at the back, oblivious to the ruckus, eyes closed, chanting in a language Sealink did not understand. From somewhere in the cavernous room, echoing among the iron girders, came the sound of perverse, arrhythmic music: bells, a reed flute, small drums. A disembodied human voice said, slowly and indistinctly, as though with much effort from a great distance, 'Bring me the kitten now. Bring her to the fire.'

Sealink had heard that voice before.

She looked wildly around the room, but the Alchemist was nowhere to be seen. How could he be? She had seen him die on the clifftops at Tintagel. There was nothing to betray any supernatural presence except for a column of milky natural nor synthetic; it was a sound that defied interpretation.

All at once there was pandemonium.

The mule skittered and the occupants of her cart shot out into the room with their fur on end. Humans clamped hands over ears and their eyes began to water. As if from nowhere, ruptured highways flickered into life on the edges of the room. A dozen cats burst out of these, followed by a dozen more, stolen away from whatever journeys they made on the wild roads of Louisiana. Drawn towards the nexus in the knacker's yard they came, fur streaming in the highway winds, dwindling second by second from their great cat forms – a leopard here, a lion there: a rosette-coated jaguar; a puma; a lynx . . .

As if the advent of these highways had released a new energy into the room, the column of light flared up suddenly, then flew apart into two separate streams. Joined only at the base these danced like two cobras; high in the air, looming up the walls and the tall, barred windows, sending grotesque shadows flying across the floor. Voices could be heard from within, echoing vaguely as if from the depths of a well, indistinct through the kitten's song; then there came a determined suspension of sound as the two streams fled back together in a sudden rush of air, to twine in violent struggle.

Isis opened her mouth wider still and the sound swelled. It wavered through a succession of eerie musical registers, finally resolving itself into a single powerful note.

The bone-fire collapsed as if it had imploded. Smoke and ash swelled into the air in billowing clouds. The dual streams of light went out, as though someone had thrown a switch. There was a great, dark roar, then a despairing voice could be heard fading to a vibration, like a ghost of itself, in the recesses of their skulls. In the sudden darkness humans wailed and ran out into the street, pursued by the larger cats.

Somehow, in all this, Shine had lost her cart. It lay now on one side, wheels spinning uselessly. The mule herself, unnerved by the scene she had interrupted, stood motionless confounded tooth and claw. She hit the first one hard on the side of his ear and bowled him over. At once, Hog leapt upon him. The second, and smaller of the two, Sealink simply fell on. He went down with a soughing sigh as the air rushed out of his lungs, then lay there in a dazed state.

The next two came and Celeste hurled herself at one, burying the few teeth she had left in its throat, while Hog and Sealink dealt with the other. Fur and howls of rage flew into the air.

They came in waves after that. Sealink fought savagely. Like the feral queen she was, she bit and tore: a whirlwind of fury.

'That's for Mousebreath!' she muttered grimly, raking the back of a lithe black tomcat now fleeing for its life. 'And that's for my lost kitten.' A patchwork cat was bowled over. 'You been destroying your own – ' she mumbled through a mouthful of grey fur ' – so that's for Azelle – ' a tortie female flew through the air. 'And that's for Candy – ' A big black and white cat was trampled underfoot.

Kiki had a large retinue. The promise of food and comfort in a city of starving ferals had brought her new recruits on a daily basis, cats whose morals, like their bodies, had been eroded by their hunger: cats who thought little of stealing kittens and betraying the presence of other cats to gain the favour of their queen. What did they care that the humans wished death upon others of their kind, so long as that enmity did not fall upon them? They had eaten well, these last few months: too well.

One by one Kiki's courtiers fell to the teeth and claws of the last free cats of New Orleans, cats carried forward only by the power of their will for revenge. Many lay still, gasping on the stone floor. Many more ran away through the open doors. Shine chased them on their way, getting in a kick here, a nip there. It was still not enough.

Celeste went down at last under the weight of three of the collared cats. Hog stood over her, teeth red with his opponents' blood; but it was impossible to withstand the tide. Before long, an exhausted Sealink found herself shoulder to shoulder with Red. Behind them, Hog and Téophine joined

What you got for a brain, honey? A ant?' She guffawed, then clapped a paw to her mouth. She winked at the calico. 'I hope you didn't – you know – get too *friendly*, down there on the boardwalk . . .'

A movement from the floor. A sudden flash of bright fur; a determined, bloodstained face. With a roar of defiance, Red launched himself at La Mère's throat. Sealink leapt for the yellow queen's back. Mother and son struck together.

That oily fur gave no purchase: Kiki shook them off like fleas, laughing all the while. As powerful as a tank, she shouldered past a helpless Téo and Hog and loomed over the golden kitten.

'Good to see you awake at last, *cher*,' she leered. 'Come to Mother.'

Isis faced her resolutely, the lines of her head as accurate as an axe. With all the courage of her parentage, she lifted her chin and spat neatly into the yellow queen's eye.

'I am not for you,' she said clearly. 'Not in this, or any other, life.'

She opened her mouth, and out came the song. It soared into the iron rafters, drew to its singer the power of the deaths suffered in that room. Many, so many: too many over the years. She felt their pain, and the power of their will to live. She drew it in; harnessing, shaping. The note swelled.

Sealink fell over, with Red beneath her. Other cats fled for the doors. Téophine dropped like a stone. Hog, with a groan, closed his eyes and slid to the floor. Shine kicked up her heels and bolted out into the street. Kiki, suddenly, clutched her head.

A highway pulsed in the air above them. There was a flash of light, and, without further warning, a cat appeared twenty feet above their heads. Plummeting groundwards, it twisted in mid-air, righted itself and struck the stone floor on all fours.

It was the Mammy.

Isis sat back, panting. The song died.

Eponine Lafeet looked around her. She gazed at Isis with her milky eyes. She smiled. '*Bonsoir, mon ange*. It is a wasn't used to having a mother, let alone one in cahoots with his mate.

'*Eh bien*, Rumby-Pumby: better start now, eh?' Celeste, leaning on Hog for support, smiled lazily.

From the fencepost behind them, the Mammy surveyed the scene with satisfaction. It was good to be back in her home town, good to have some of her own to look after again. A couple of dozen ferals and a few homeless domestic cats had made their way across the city to the boardwalk. She recognized some as former members of her daughter's retinue; but the malice had gone out of their eyes, just as the worst of the madness had gone out of the city. Two large-furred tabbies had arrived just that morning, bearing, respectively, a shrimp and a crab-claw, heads bowed; rather shamefaced. And later that day she had watched, from a safe place, as a woman she remembered as Rita came down to the Moonwalk, followed cautiously by a yellow dog, to empty cans of strong-smelling tuna-fish in the old place by the steps.

Eponine Lafeet smiled. It was a start. A good start.

She waved the calico cat and her golden charge on their way.

the neglected rear section of the churchyard – where the graves were tossed like little boats on a sea of the tangled grass, like no other grass in the world, that mats all church-yards – and over the wall into a rather neat garden, with clumps of yellow poppies.

'Oh, I know very well what you think,' she chided him before he could answer. 'You think, "This fragile spinster". You think, "This pet cat who came from nowhere in a furrier's van". You think, "However did she make herself the village queen?" Well, I wonder that myself sometimes!'

'I think you are all steel underneath, and always were,' was Animal X's quiet reply.

'It's not a bit of use you speaking,' she said irritably.

At that moment, two houseflies, borne on some ecstatic updraught of which they were only partly aware, blundered onto the warm stone in front of her and began immediately to copulate. Locked together in that way, they looked like an iridescent enamel brooch in the sunlight. Every so often they buzzed groggily and lurched into a new position. Cottonreel stood up, stretched, and examined them lazily.

'I don't think I could eat them while they were doing that,' she said. 'Do you? It seems unfair.'

She dabbed at them until they flew away.

Suddenly she said, 'You'll leave us soon, Animal X. Oh, no, don't protest. You pretend to be calm, but you are the most driven cat I ever met.' She stared out over the treetops. 'Though perhaps not the angriest,' she continued in a softer voice. And then, 'Will you do me a favour as you go about the world? Will you look out for a black cat?'

She ran her eyes over Animal X.

'He is rather bigger than you, if that's possible. Long-haired, and with a great tangled mane. I only met him the once. He was very dirty, rather fine and gentle yet quick to act on behalf of weaker animals. If you ever see a cat like that on your journeys,' she said, 'remind him of me, will you? Tell him that Cottonreel sends her love.'

Later she said, 'Is it me, or is it a little cooler? Shall we go down?' And then, on the stairs, 'You will be careful with Amelie's feelings, won't you?'

'Oh he's an entertainment in his own right, that cat!'

But if he had exchanged cheese for friends, food was still the axis of Stilton's life. He had eaten so many new things! He described them to Animal X, one by one. 'Bread and milk, now,' he sighed. 'That's quite something the first time you have it. Then somehow you can have enough of it.'

He looked thoughtful for a minute. Then he brightened up. 'And as for seafood cocktail with coldwater shrimp! Have you ever had that? As Runcer always says, "Seafood cocktail. That'll make your bowels come up." It slips down well, a bit of the old seafood cocktail. It really hits the spot—'

'So you're happy here,' interrupted Animal X.

Stilton looked puzzled.

'I suppose I am,' he acknowledged, as if Animal X had shown him something new about himself. Then he laughed. 'But do you know, there are nights I wake up and miss the cabinet?'

Animal X said he found this hard to believe.

'That wasn't a good place for cats,' he pointed out.

'Oh, I don't know,' said Stilton. 'There was some real companionship. And the stories we told one another! Those weren't such bad days.'

'Perhaps not,' said Animal X. 'Perhaps they weren't. Think how bad the food was, though.' While to himself he said, 'Stilton is beginning to forget: that is how I know he is cured.'

He said, 'I was thinking of leaving soon.'

Stilton stood blinking at him in the sunlight.

At night Animal X watched the chains of laboratory cats, still a little bemused by the change in their lives, wandering through the moonlight. Their eyes were like small oval lights in the fields down near the water. Sometimes they were like a living carpet, wheeling down from the woods to silently fill the village street. They had been released, he thought: but not released. They were waiting for something more. He was like that. He saw and heard with absolute clarity, he could see dew form on a leaf: but

'I am leaving soon,' he said.

'You would be bound to go. To find the sea.'

'Will you come with me?'

'No,' she said, as if it was a decision she had made some time ago. 'Part of me would like to. But something is happening in the world. Is it good or bad? Who knows what it will mean to all these half-healed cats?' She turned to face him. 'I want to be here when it happens.'

She said, 'They will still need my help.'

'I knew you wouldn't come,' said Animal X.

'Part of me would like to,' repeated Amelie. She said. 'I hope you find what you want, and that your life is a good one.'

'Perhaps I'll come back and see you.'

She laughed.

'Perhaps you will,' she said.

He left with the kitten a few days later, in the undecided light of early morning. A few birds sang. Later, the air would glitter: now it was dove-grey, and so damp as to be palpable, an air on the edge of being mist, through which had recently fallen a steady drenching rain. Stilton came out of his chicken hutch to say goodbye to them, and they all three stood looking awkwardly at one another for a moment. The kitten lurched unhappily about, bumping into the others, licking Stilton's head one minute, hissing at him the next, in the confusion of whatever it was feeling. Then Animal X, with too many things to say and no way of saying any of them, rubbed his cheek against his old friend's and told him, 'I'll miss you.'

'I'll miss you too,' said Stilton.

'It's best you stay, though.'

'It's best I stay. I never had a life before.'

'You'll be happy here.'

They stared at one another for a moment longer, then Animal X turned resolutely away.

He said, 'I have to go now.'

He said, 'The kitten is very disturbed now.'

'Goodbye,' called Stilton. 'Goodbye!'

He followed them along the street, still calling,

sleep to find a half-grown rabbit staring him straight in the face, one agitated blowfly crawling over its glazed eye. After that, despite its obvious limitations, the kitten became an efficient, indeed merciless, hunter. Its movements retained an adolescent touch of exaggeration. But there was killing torsion pent up in the flex and spring of its body. Rage, unalloyed and barely diverted, informed the freeze into immobility, the sudden hyperbolic leap above the tangled bracken. Animal X winced at its violence: yet found himself recipient of an embarrassment of riches. One evening a pile of voles, an entire family of mice wiped out the next. The kitten never touched anything it brought him, so he had no idea what it was eating; but he had already seen it bring down a full-grown pigeon which was five feet from the ground and flying hard when the golden jaws closed on its neck.

Mile flowed seamlessly into mile. They rarely strayed from the river. But the surrounding land rose steadily until no river-bank remained worth speaking of; and they were forced to walk far above the water where dwarf oak and broken walls clung to steep ground, and a system of green lanes ushered them out onto spacious upland lawn, sheep-cropped, studded with tormentil, drenched in light.

Outcrops of rose-pink rock stood up out of the rolling turf, quartz-veined, surrounded by dense, wind-sculpted stands of gorse. The air was different up there: it went lively, unfixed, free. There was such a sudden sense of space. Animal X stared around. 'We're very high up,' he thought. 'But that's not it.' The turf stretched away; the sky was so bright it seemed to go on for ever; at the junction of the two lay a broad, supple, glittering band of silver. Then, racing towards him out of the dazzle and haze, a huge bird! It hovered for a moment, and swung away on the wind and disappeared, and all he had left was an image of its cruciform shape, its snowy body and strong yellow beak, its forlorn cry. 'You can see further there,' he remembered Amelie saying. 'And there are birds that make the loneliest noise you have ever heard.'

'We're at the sea,' thought Animal X.

The kitten came and stood beside him.

'Hello?' said Animal X.

Birds flew up carking and cawing from their hidden roosts in the granite, their wings like black rags on a hot wind. They circled above his head. Like the light, they had been nestled down inside things all along, waiting for him to arrive in this place. 'The crows!' thought Animal X. 'The crows!'

He felt the light try its strength, and leap out of the stones and flicker around his head. He flattened his ears and ran for it. Where could he go? Halfway to nowhere the fuse burned out. Green fire laced the gorse without consuming it. Flames roared silently across the turf, gathering into shapes he didn't want to acknowledge. The crows wheeled and sideslipped above him, dipping down to strike at his head, their cries redoubled, plangent, coarse, full of some hateful irony. Fear drove him towards the place where the land finished, where the huge ocean awaited him, grey and lavender, touched with silver. Then he was right on the lip of it all in the reek of salt and iodine, staring down a hundred feet at rocks, foam, booming and turmoil far below. The land shook with every wave. Spray shot up in rainbow arcs. It was more water than he could ever have imagined. Animal X didn't care.

'I've seen enough now,' he thought. 'I've seen too much.' And with a quiet sense of relief he threw himself over the edge. He would fall now. He would give himself up to it. He would escape the crows and whatever they were trying to make him understand. As he fell he had a brief, puzzling glimpse of something glorious and golden. Its jaws closed firmly on his neck, and he went quickly away from himself and everything else –

– to dream of a cat which lay beside a cold river.

It was morning, early. Winter greyed the air between the elder saplings; the tangled willows put up the undersides of their leaves in the breeze; dead bramble suckers and ground ivy thickened the river-banks. The water was gelid – clear, yet coloured at the same time, as very cold water often is, a kind of light green-grey. Its surface was dimpled with eddies. Hidden currents tugged, strong and amiable, at a

299

sodden fur. It was cold, large rain; the river-banks were like sponges with it. The crows returned, and – inch by inch, less quarrelsome now, more focused – moved upon their meal. Towards noon, when a faint yellow sun began to be visible behind the clouds, two or three of them became too hungry to wait any longer. They darted forward, ready to hammer at the cat with their big black beaks. Crows will hammer all day long to get what they want, work for ever over a bit of bone, the rag of a lamb in a bare field. Sensing something of this, the cat dragged itself awake again. Its eyes were mismatched, one blue, one a strange sodium-orange more fitted to city streets than country lanes. Through them the cat saw painful flashes and arcs of sunlight, mixed up with sleek, jostling, intelligent heads. A crow can hammer all the way to the heart of things if necessary – get the good bits before they go cold. The cat gathered the last of its strength. It dragged itself partway out of the encumbering plastic bag and went for its tormentors, teeth and claws bared. 'Cark! Aaargh!' they sneered, from the safety of the air. A crow always has the last word. The cat looked up, in anger and fear. Then, the remains of the supermarket bag still trailing from one rear leg, it made off at a kind of lumbering trot along the muddy bank and up onto the nearest road where, after walking for about a mile, it was brought down again by its wounds.

Half an hour passed. The sun had broken through. The cat lay in the gutter near some trees, not thinking much. The supermarket bag fluttered idly. A vehicle came into view. It was a white-panel van with rust marks around the door-sills. It passed the cat at high speed, then stopped suddenly. Two men dressed in light blue overalls got out and, talking in low voices, walked back to where the cat lay in the gutter. They looked down thoughtfully, and one of them began to pull on a pair of thick, worn leather gloves.

'Any good?'

'Nah. It's well stuffed, this one.'

'It's alive.'

'That's about all you can say. What are they going to do with it in this condition?'

'Well, that's heartening,' said Animal X. There was a silence. 'Could you speak all along, then?' he said. 'I wondered if you could speak, all along.'

'After what happened to me,' the kitten said, 'after the indignity of what they did to me in that place—' It seemed to lose its thread, and for some seconds stared out to sea. Then it began again. 'Human beings snatched me from my sisters. I was dragged under the earth and stuffed in a sack. They took me away in a boat and then some filthy vehicle brought me to that place. They took my eye!' it cried bitterly. 'They took my eye, they took Stilton's wits, they took your memory! After what they did to us all in that place, my throat would not speak.' And then, in wonder, 'It would not speak, however hard I tried, until I was home again.'

'They took nothing from me,' said Animal X gently. 'I took my own memory away because I wasn't ready to face it.' As he spoke, he was studying the clifftop with new interest. There were pools of ruffled water among the rocks; tufts of salty grass; not much else. 'I can't see how a cat lives in this wind,' he said. 'How does a cat get a living here? You live here?'

'Near her. My name is Odin, and I am a prince. I believe we are all in terrible danger. Will you help me find my mother, the Queen? I promise she is near.'

He sniffed the air.

'Home is so close,' he said quietly. 'Over that headland, or the next.'

As soon as he heard the word 'Queen', the healing of Animal X was complete. He laughed softly to himself. 'I remember *that* one,' he thought: 'I remember the tongue on her!' He knew who he was now. He knew the meaning of the crow-dream stitched like a loop into the middle of his life. He understood the irony of his journey to this clifftop; he remembered his friends; he wondered what had become of the world he knew. He was filled with energy when he thought about it. 'It must have worked out, one way or another,' he told himself. 'All that. It must be gone like a dream now. Something new will be going on now.' He

XIX

The Beautiful Friend

The return journey was difficult and slow.

Well-known roads proved impassable, or were simply no longer there; those that still worked had turned into a maze of seeping corridors through nothing, opening suddenly onto bleak woods under grey, mucous airs, in country no-one ever visited. Leonora, compelled by each impasse to invent ever more complex dances, grew tired and muddled. The New Majicou, goaded by anxieties he would not explain, chafed at each delay, lost his patience with her, and tried to force passage where none existed. As a result, they lost their way. Later, at some point of decision so subtle they were past it before either of them guessed, they lost Loves A Dustbin and the New Black King too. Back by the sea at last, still alone, they found the night old, the moon down, squalls of cold rain racing landward across the bay.

Leo said they were lucky to have arrived home at all. That was her opinion, anyway.

She stuck her head into the familiar hole at the base of the oceanarium doors. Then she backed out again very suddenly without saying anything.

This is what she had seen inside:

A dozen verminous tomcats thrown into silhouette by the fish-tank's brilliant glare, which, pouring between them, threw their elongated black shadows across the concrete floor and up the peeling walls. They sat in a half-circle idly stripping their claws (already as sharp as straight razors), scratching their foul ears, or staring with greedy puzzlement into the aquarium at the silent, mysterious, unreachable world within. Between them and the tank they had trapped Pertelot Fitzwilliam of Hi-Fashion, Queen of Cats. Her head

'I should have asked: "Is there a highway entrance inside the House of Uroum Bashou?"'

'And is there?'

'No.'

'So?'

'Cats are larger than life when they leave the Old Changing Way: but they always return to normal in a minute or two. So how does Kater Murr maintain himself as the great brass animal you encountered, first in the Reading Cat's kitchen and later on his stairs? If I had thought about that, instead of showing off to you – '

He sighed.

'Kater Murr has a line of power,' he was forced to admit, 'the other end of which leads to the Alchemist.'

'What are we going to do?' demanded Leonora.

'Think for a moment.'

'No! No! My mother is in there! Pertelot and Cy are in there!'

'Yet if we rush in now, all will be lost. Kater Murr has achieved less than he imagines. The Alchemist has not so much empowered him as prepared him, like any other proxy, for some undisclosed purpose. Without his master, he could not stand against me for long—'

'Then go in and deal with him!' interrupted Leonora. 'You're the Majicou.'

' – yet if I challenge him directly he will kill your mother before I can kill him,' he went on gently. 'Do you want that? I only know I would not like to lose Cy that way.'

Even as he spoke, Leonora was darting past him to squirm through the hole at the base of the doors. From inside he heard her mutter, 'Leave it to Leonora, as usual.'

And then, 'Tag?'

'Oh Leonora, Leonora,' he said.

It was hard to hide in the oceanarium. Since the only object in it was the giant glass tank, and since the lamp was positioned directly above that, there weren't even many fixed shadows to be found: and they were all associated with the spiral staircase. Tag and Leo kept in among them, as far

Kater Murr purred. His outline flickered.

'Come to Kater Murr my dear. You're enough to make anyone feel brand-new.'

At this, Tag told Leonora, 'Stay here if you want to live!' and stepped out of the shadows.

'Empty speech, Kater Murr,' he said.

Kater Murr became very still.

'Is there someone else in here with me?' he asked his companions. 'I thought I heard someone speak.'

The tomcats stared at him then at one another, anxious to please but too full of testosterone to know what was happening.

'Was it,' Kater Murr wondered, 'a fish?'

'You know me, Kater Murr,' said Tag. 'I am the Majicou.'

Kater Murr stared hard at a shoal of mackerel. They moved uneasily behind the glass. 'I think it was that one there,' he said. 'That was the speaking fish.'

'You know me, Kater Murr.'

Slowly, slowly, Kater Murr turned his head until he was able to look at Tag out of one amber eye. Then he said, 'I don't need to know anyone now.'

He said, 'Oh, I saw you at the Library (your head was in a book, but you can't read), listening to his endless boring stories, day after day. It was always "the Reading Cat knows this, the Reading Cat knows that," but what is reading anyway? Reading is not so difficult. *Kater Murr* learned to read. Oh yes he did! But Kater Murr learned *what* to read. Kater Murr is a successful cat. Kater Murr has important friends—'

'Kater Murr is nothing,' said Tag. 'You killed the Reading Cat out of jealousy. Had you already found your way to the room beneath the copper dome? I think you had. I think that was where you were taught to read. Kater Murr is a pet cat, who dabbled where he had no understanding. Kater Murr is still a doorkeeper.'

He paused.

'Though now he keeps the Alchemist's door,' he said.

limp had quite vanished. Sizing up the situation in an instant, these two drove straight towards the Queen. Tag stared at them. How had the situation deteriorated so fast? He shrugged, and sprang at Kater Murr. The astonished doorkeeper, bowled over in a reeking heap, squirmed and paddled himself away, then returned and took a good hold of Tag's cheek below the left eye. Their heads went back briefly and they spat in one another's faces and with that everything came apart for good. It was like a signal. Cy jumped up and began worrying the haunch of Kater Murr. Pertelot and her daughter, their eyes glittering with malice, addressed themselves to his astonished lieutenants. Soon the oceanarium was a mêlée of screeching cats and flying fur, at the centre of which pounced and darted a single large dog-fox, giving much better than he got. Left to itself, despite the uneven numbers, this situation could only have developed in one way – several of the tomcats were already thinking about leaving. But Kater Murr was no ordinary cat –

Some blow of Tag's had sent him reeling. Trying to escape another, he ran full tilt into the fish-tank and slid down it with his cheek pressed to the glass. When he came to rest, the eye on that side had closed for good. The other had a glazed look.

He groaned.

'Kater Murr knows a thing or two,' he said.

His outline wavered. The air around him crackled and spat. Every cat present felt its hair stand on end. They stopped fighting and regarded one another warily, while large slow bluish sparks, wandering aimlessly about at head-height, discharged themselves in perfect silence against the spiral stairs. Kater Murr tried to get up. He convulsed. He seemed to shoot out from himself in all directions at once, and the assembled cats felt him *pass through* them like a ripple in the air. Then he was gone, and in his place had appeared the dream-cat, the avatar, the gatekeeper's savage icon of himself. It was the size of a small horse. Its fur was coarse and orange. Black markings chased each other down its sides like drawings of flames. Every bunch-and-pull of its muscles brought forth a reek of ammonia, pheromones and paw was spread and displayed, an attitude struck then folded. There was a sudden, coughing snarl, then a flurry of violence. It was hard to see what was happening through the shifting veils of snow. Two huge bodies collided with a groan like cars in a fog, disengaged immediately, began to pace around one another once more, turning this way and that in anticipation of some advantage lost even as it was gained. Suddenly they embraced again, less briefly. They writhed and fell. Hind claws raked and ripped, fur flew like raw and rusty wire. Then they were up and pacing restlessly again, panting for breath, trembling with blood-chemicals, looking for an opening. But now Kater Murr seemed quite blind.

'Go home, Kater Murr. Be a cat.'

'Did I hear someone speak?'

To the watchers, everything seemed confused, too quick, too real. It was finished in an instant. Sabre teeth flashed across a bared orange throat. Blood-heat warmed the air. Kater Murr looked surprised. 'Kater Murr is a cat among cats,' he said, watching his life stream away into the ice. 'His body hurts, but what does he care?'

His rank smell overpowered everything for a moment – then another smell, of musk and winter, powder snow on an icy wind, washed it away. There was a distant, fading roar.

The watching animals shivered. ('I didn't want him to die,' whispered Leonora Whitstand Merril. 'He was a cat like us.') The next time they looked, the oceanarium had reassembled itself around them. It was warm and dry. The fish circled endlessly in the heat of the electric lamp. The only sign that anything had changed was the corpse of Kater Murr, which lay sodden and used-looking, like a doormat in the rain, a little way away from the foot of the spiral stairs. His lieutenants had seized the day, and were gone.

'Wow,' breathed Cy. 'Home again!'

The fox looked around, shook himself suddenly and went to the doors to keep an eye on the night. 'Cats!' he was thinking. 'What can you say?'

One by one, they relaxed. The New Majicou had transported them briefly to some country of his own. It had been

The cats slept in a heap: two bodies here curled yin and yang – two heads there resting on the same flank – more paws than you could imagine. The fox watched over them for a while, grinning his feral grin as he tried to work out who was connected to what; then, giving up, went off to doze on his own by the door, thinking, 'I rather like them. But I'd prefer cubs.' While, behind the glass, exalted by the light pouring down, the fishes turned and danced. All was calm in the oceanarium until, perhaps two hours before dawn, Kater Murr's bedraggled remains began to stir.

It was some internal rearrangement, the fox thought, some contraction of the ligaments: the faint paradoxical gestures of rigor. A paw twitched. The stuffed-looking head, with its glassy eyes and snaggle-teeth, seemed to settle minutely. That would have been that for an ordinary cat – but not for Kater Murr. His outline seemed to shift. The air around him flexed and creaked. Suddenly, the fox's mouth was filled with a bad taste. Head low and hackles stiff, he approached the corpse. Warm draughts curled round it briefly, lifting dust into his eyes.

'What's this?' he asked himself.

He thought he had better alert the New Majicou: but, as soon as he turned away from the corpse, a polite cough came from behind him, then another noise which, once it had begun, went on and on –

The cats woke up to find him darting round them in desperation, nipping at their ears, their noses, their tails, yelping, 'Wake up! Wake up!' They jumped to their feet, fur on end, blinking in sleepy alarm. The electric light pulsed slowly and nauseously; while, inside the tank itself, lightning seemed to flicker as the panicked fish twisted to and fro. 'Wake up!' All they could tell was that the half-dark was full of the drone of some faulty machine. A strong, insistent wind, rattling and banging at the oceanarium doors until it tore them open, deafened the cats and made them stagger. A stinging litter of plastic straws, cigarette-ends, grit, sheets of newspaper and discarded fast-food cartons blew into their faces, to whirl past and be sucked up loose whirl of litter you might see at any street corner on a windy day. Then a note or two of music was played, on reeds and finger-drums, and a human figure became visible. 'Bring me your kittens,' the figure said. 'Bring me all the kittens.' Mutilated in some way, and wearing a mask, it held its arms in stiff, hieratic positions. There was a deep, hollow groan of pain, and a different voice said clearly, 'Tag, we can still defeat him if we keep our heads.'

Tag withdrew hastily. The last thing he saw was Kater Murr, who could still be made out at the toe of the vortex, where it tapered down to a single point gliding here and there at random an inch or so above the dead cat's fur. Tag expected to see him sucked up like everything else, but he simply lay there while it buzzed and groaned above him, his teeth drawn back in a terrible grin.

'This was what he wanted,' the grin seemed to say. 'Kater Murr was no ordinary thing.'

Five cats and a fox stood above a seaside town in the hour before dawn, waiting to see what would come next. The sky above the bay was full of rushing cobalt blue cloud, a layer of grey impasto obscuring its junction with the sea. There were no lights in the cottages that tumbled away down the windy hill to the harbour.

'Cold here,' said Cy to Tag. She looked up at him. 'Get closer,' she ordered. When he didn't reply, she purred anyway. 'Hey, don't worry, Ace,' she advised him. 'It'll all come out in the wash. Get it?'

He stared at her.

'I'll never understand you,' he said.

She wriggled with pleasure.

'What's to understand?' she said. 'Girls just want to have fun.' She looked down at the oceanarium. 'It's a roary old night,' she said grimly.

'It is,' said Tag.

He left her for a moment and went to talk to Ragnar and the fox. 'There isn't much cover here,' he said, staring across the hilltop. It was desolate and exposed – tourist-worn grass, one or two concrete benches, a litter-bin, some small a slate roof and was already out of sight. But it was coming towards them, whatever it was –

'Look now!' urged Pertelot. 'See? Rags, Mercury, can you see?'

– and, as it came closer, its movements resolved into the distinctive body language of a hurrying cat: the steep leap up onto the wall, the quick deft padding run extended into a graceful arc, the scuttle across rain-blackened granite setts. Even so, at that distance nothing was certain except that these actions had been performed. No-one – they were all watching expectantly now – had yet seen the cat that performed them. Then the fox said, 'There, by the base of that wall. Two of them!' After a moment he added, 'They know what they're doing.'

There they were, moving fast and agile through the gale and the flying wrack, giving a wide berth to the oceanarium, keeping to the lee of things when they could. They were outdoor cats, lean and muscular, hard as nails. They were clearly a team, but one was always a little ahead of the other, stopping and waiting briefly before running on, as if it alone knew the way.

Larger but more lightly-built, with long and rangy legs, it had a short thick pelt which shone a kind of dull gold in the dirty light. Catching sight of the cats on the hill, and suddenly unable to contain itself any longer, it left its companion behind at last and came bounding up towards them, calling out their names. For their part, they observed with sadness its missing eye, but marked the power of its limbs, the joy and energy in every stride –

Then Pertelot was turning in excited circles, calling, 'Odin! It's Odin! Oh Rags, oh everyone, look. Do look!'

The first of the lost kittens had come home.

Some years before, an autumn storm had torn two score Welsh slates from the seaward side of the oceanarium roof. The panels of corrugated iron which had replaced them – painted first black and then a curious cheap aquamarine colour soon streaked with rust – were now trying to take flight in their turn, screeching and rattling and tearing their efforts would have rolled the world along beneath them, and their joy reclaimed the bleak little night-time hilltop and made it a park.

It was such a reunion! But the New Majicou stood apart from it all, looking puzzledly down the hill. Just outside the reach of the last good street-lamp, where the cottages petered out and the grass began, Odin's companion waited alone, a shadowy figure blinking uncertainly in the dim light.

'Won't you come up?' he invited.

No answer.

He felt a sudden dread.

'It was good of you to bring the kitten home,' he said.

Still no answer.

'He says you know us. He says you once knew Pertelot Fitzwilliam.'

Silence.

'Won't you come up and let us thank you?'

Only silence.

'Then I'll come down,' said Tag.

'Nah, nah,' said a quiet voice. 'No need for that. I was a bit shy, that's all. I'm all right now. No need for you to come down.'

Out of the shadows stepped a cat the colour of a shellac comb. His coat was so heavily mottled and patterned, so dark in places, as to be almost black. The fur itself was very short and coarse, with a suspicion of a curl. One of his eyes was a frank and open speedwell blue, the other was the colour of sodium light. Both were framed by the grey, ridged scar tissue of the compulsive street-fighter, and despite his numerous old wounds he still moved with a heavy, rolling grace.

Tag stared.

'You're dead,' he whispered.

Mousebreath looked down at himself.

'Nah mate,' he said. 'I'm not.'

He said, 'It was touch an' go for a bit though, I'll say that.'

He studied Tag out of his blue eye.

Every stone was outlined in light as it separated gently from the stones around it. The noise ran rapidly up to a whine so high-pitched you could barely detect it. At the instant it snapped into inaudibility, there was a soft contemptuous 'Pah!' as of expelled breath, and the building blew apart. The cats were bowled over by the force of it. Stone blocks, broken slates, and bits of timber the size of railway sleepers rained down, thudding deep into the earth around them. They took shelter under a concrete bench, and found the fox already in possession.

'Look at that,' he said disgustedly.

There was just enough light left to see the fish-tank, standing complete and undamaged on its circular concrete base. A flicker of motion here and there inside suggested that its inhabitants, though surprised, remained mobile and in their proper element.

'How does that happen?' said the fox. 'How does a thing like that happen?'

'Ask yourself what has happened to the whirlwind,' advised the New Majicou irritably. 'We will never be safe if all this is not brought to an end!'

No more objects fell. One by one the animals pulled themselves out from under the bench and looked around cautiously. They looked inland. Nothing. They looked out to sea. Nothing there, either. Out in the bay a light breeze had got up and was blowing towards them. It smelled of dawn, though the eastern sky remained dark.

'We are OK now, I think,' declared Ragnar.

The earth in front of him shook and rumbled. Out of it, with a grinding noise like ancient machinery, rose two figures.

Vast and silent, as posed and hieratic as the stone giants in an Egyptian temple, they loomed up motionless against the sky, Majicou and the Alchemist, the wise black cat and his erstwhile master. The cat's tail lashed. The Alchemist's rags fluttered a little in the wind. They seemed uncertain. They had been a long time in their own domain, bound one to the other. They had been much under the earth, in the darkness, unwilling to give up. They were unfamiliar with and Leonora – as if they were entering a building, as if some real shelter might be had from him; and indeed the wind did seem to abate a little in the lee of his warm body. The dustbin fox gave him a strange, long, yellow-eyed look –

'Take care, my friend!' he warned. 'You have done this too often already!'

– and tucked in behind. The last to come was Cy the tabby. She rubbed her head against him and purred so loudly he could hear her above the gathering storm.

'I always had faith in you, Ace,' she said. 'Don't let me down now.'

Tag laughed.

'Tuck in!' he cried. 'And look away!'

There was a crash of thunder and a smell of distant snow.

Arriving disoriented and irritable after her recent hometown travails, Sealink the calico regarded the scene on the hilltop with disbelief.

She had enjoyed the flight – when had she not enjoyed a flight? – but not the grim and tiring journey from the airport, struggling like an insect in the shredded web of the Old Changing Way. Isis, preoccupied and driven and sometimes not what you would call good company, had sung them through the difficulties – an act in itself less than comforting. Her music often engaged something eerie in the world. To be frank, it set your teeth on edge. Despite all that, though, and despite the kitten's disappointment when she found her Tintagel home abandoned, they had made it. Where they had made it to was another matter.

'It looked like hell,' she would say later. 'And, to tell the truth, so did you guys.'

The symbol which – from Egyptian tomb to Louisiana swamp to Tintagel cave – had presided over every turn of these events, now pulsed on and off in the pre-dawn sky like neon outside a fish-and-chip shop. Dimly and intermittently revealed by this eerie half-light, the top of the hill, with its half-buried lumps of fallen masonry, seemed like the surface of the moon; while the remains of the oceanarium resembled some recent, disputed archaeological find.

XX

Green World

But Isis wasn't listening. She had run off to join Odin and Leo.

'Honey,' Sealink began, 'I don't think—'

Too late.

Everything hung for an instant on the edge of disaster, then toppled over.

Isis called out to her brother and sister. Hearing her voice but unable to see her, Odin and Leo abandoned the lee of the white tiger and ran about aimlessly through the wrack.

'*I'll have them all now,*' the vortex told itself.

Isis froze, one forepaw lifted. She glanced desperately this way and that.

At the last minute, as the whirlwind bent towards her, Mercurius Realtime DeNeuve reared up between them, offering his iron claws –

Deprived of shelter by this manoeuvre, the remaining cats scattered and went to ground in shallow scoops and pockets in the exposed pink granite bedrock. There, they hung on grimly. They would have to endure, they supposed. They tried, as cats do when things have gone too far, to hunch down inside themselves and persist.

Sealink, watching in a kind of paralysis, unable to think of anything at all to do to help her old friends, imagined for a moment she could see a tortoiseshell tom among them. Her heart leapt: but it was only the dustbin fox after all, his coat mottled with dirt. Who else might be there was hard to tell, though she thought she saw Ragnar Gustaffson, trying with some success to shelter his Queen.

'Steady, girl,' she warned herself. 'No use folding now. This is an extreme situation – '

watching. 'And this is how I do it when they hide in the long grass. See? More height in the jump, and bring your weight down behind your front paws. Like this!'

They observed this demonstration gravely.

They exchanged a long confidential glance, as if to say, Yes, that is how to hunt. But now this. Look! Listen!'

Then Leonora Whitstand Merril began to dance, and Isis began to sing, and the hunt and the dance and the song wove a kind of pattern into the air around them. It was long and intricate, and the threads in it were made of gold and blood and all the things cats have ever done. And this is some of the meaning of it (because it is still being sung):

Eat, bear kittens, sing the song of the cat in the night. This is a grasshopper, this is a mouse, but this only a bit of grass in a dry wind. These are the leaves of the trees and the birds among them (which also sing). This is how to change direction at full speed – you may need that trick sooner than you think. Hush! That is a kitten, lost in the dark; and this is the sound the lark makes as she rises through the morning (never eat her feet). This is how we were in Nubia, and then in Egypt. Men welcomed us. The Nile comforted us. Her pigeons were in our mouths –

It was less a song, or a dance, or a practice for the hunt, than a tapestry, the *tapetum lucidum* of the *felidae*. The task of weaving it brought the kittens closer and closer together until they were facing one another from the points of a triangle again. A ripple seemed to pass through them. A shaft of light struck down from above. Their images were progressively overlaid, shimmering like cats seen through heat haze on a summer morning. Suddenly, they had slipped into one another, and a single animal stood where three had been. It looked back at its parents, then turned and loped away into its own dance and vanished.

Only the bright tapestry remained, intricating itself across the hilltop, febrile and tenuous, as if the very air were gilded with the life of cats.

Sealink looked up.

We know how Animal X saw her. Since his experience in the laboratory, She had rushed in upon him day by day as a green fire, and taken him in the jaws of love.

But the dustbin fox said he saw this: shapes perhaps not even animal, but moving with the fluid violence of leopards, glorious unassuaged green forms like archangels, flowing through the world determined to change it. Was it the Great Cat herself, or only her servants? *Who knows?* he asked himself: *She is the world.* It made him remember why he had thrown in his lot with the Old Majicou, so many years ago. 'In that moment I remembered,' he was to say later, 'what we were trying to accomplish. But I still wept for Francine, wasted in someone else's war.'

As for Cy the tabby: no-one ever knew what she saw.

'I mean,' she tried to explain later, 'now you see it, now you don't. You know? It's hidden in the shapes of things. It's crouched in the bus shelter. It lies in wait in the curve of the bay. What's familiar, you see it new. Over and out, Ace: is that enough for you? Anything you look at's true!'

And what Ragnar and Pertelot saw was this:

A great triangle of light – the signature of their children, made to bring forth something even stranger than themselves – and, dawning at its apex, a light the colour of peach and amber. Inside that light, curled in the vast sleep of time yet wakeful as the day, the Great Cat herself, the Mother of everything, the green dream that beats like a heart at the heart of the world. They knew her by her body, which is hill and bleak mountain, jungle and forest, and at the same time home and hearth. They knew her by that endless rumbling purr which is the sound of the world, the deep engines of the weather, the wind and the wave and the ocean the wave plays upon, and everything under the ocean, even to the deep halls of the fish. They knew her by her fur, which is a transforming fire, green on the edge of gold. They knew her by her seasons, which come and go. They knew her by her delight in every kitten, every scuttling mouse, every fallen leaf: and She knew them.

She opened her silver eye.

Only the Great Cat remained. Green as jade, gold as the sun, She left the King and Queen, and flickered like flames across the hilltop and wove her way into the heart of the storm, where She sat down suddenly and began to clean her paws. The air boomed and pulsed around her. Long streamers of cobalt-coloured detritus were pulled out between earth and sky, twisting and interleaving themselves. Blue lightning flared and banged, and out to sea the wind ripped the grey waves to spray. The ground shook. The whirlwind loomed up –

'Be still now,' She commanded.

She said, 'Come to me now, both of you, and be still.'

But the whirlwind would not obey. The two beings inside it raged across the hilltop, out to sea and back again. They would not even answer. They wanted nothing She could offer. They were the Opposites, the sibling rivals, the dynamo of a vanishing age. They only wanted the struggle. After three hundred years, they had forgotten almost everything else.

The Great Cat laughed.

'The wild and the tame are only names for the same thing,' She chided them.

'Will you come to me?' She said gently.

They would not. Why should they humble themselves in that way? (Though each would like to humble the other.) They tore up the bedrock and threw it about.

'It has been a long time, I know,' She said.

She said, 'Aren't you tired?'

At this, the winds died so suddenly that the world ached with silence. They *were* tired. They were old. As they wavered, so did the vortex. Its rate of spin decreased, a shudder passed through it. It toppled and lost coherence. There was a long pause. Then the air breathed a sigh of relief, and began to clarify itself, like liquid in a glass. Everything which had been suspended, from mica dust to roofing slates, from cigarette packs to old car tyres, was released. The sky filled with objects, caught in a reluctant, dreamy, slow-motion fall.

'I absolve you,' said the Great Cat.

laughed. 'Well, perhaps I would,' She said. 'They're perfect enough—'

'I have always thought so,' agreed the King of Cats complacently.

'Rags!' his wife admonished him.

' – but watch!' finished the Great Cat.

There was a curious twist of light in the air beside her. Out of it to stand by her side, deep-chested and lithe, its legs impossibly thin and elegant, its strange long back curving away from high pointed shoulder to rangy haunch, came the Golden Cat. Its eyes were unearthly.

'Here they are,' She said. 'I give them back to you, three kittens in one. Odin the hunter, with his dance of death. Isis, who stands for resurrection, protection, reincarnation, and song enough to wake the dead. Impetuous Leonora, whose joy is in the moment: she dances the dance of life. This is your child and mine,' She told the King and Queen. 'It is the child of the time to come. The birth of this cat was planned long before the white ship landed your forbears at Tintagel. See how it will run, through all the next age of the world. Look!' She said. 'Oh, look!' A highway was opened before them, and the Golden Cat ran away down it with long, graceful, tireless strides. At the same time, it was somehow running towards them, shifting and changing into Odin and Isis and Leonora Whitstand Merril as it came.

'Mother!' cried Leonora. 'Tell Odin I was right! *They were down there all the time!*'

'This is the problem with daughters,' said Ragnar Gustaffson. 'They always have to quibble.'

'I have no answer to that,' the Great Cat told him. 'I was a daughter myself.' And She began to fade away into her own dream. 'Your lives were broken, but now they are mended,' She told them. 'Run!' She said. 'I will always be with you now. Run and eat!' She said, 'You are *all* Golden Cats.'

And then, when only her voice was left in the jasmine-scented air, barely distinguishable from the soft sound of water in the hidden gardens of the Nile, She advised them

The tabby pushed her way between them.

'You let me down!' she cried. 'You let me down!' It wasn't clear which one of them she meant. She touched the side of Tag's face gently with one paw. 'Come back!' she said. 'You come back now!' For the twentieth time since she had found him, she shut her eyes, put her mouth close to his nose, and exhaled sharply into his nostrils.

Nothing.

'This stuff is broke,' she said, looking up at Ragnar and Pertelot as if it was their fault. 'I was woke by it myself enough times before. Now it just don't work, when I know it should!'

'Nothing works,' the fox said.

Without turning round, he added, 'Life can be very remote. It can hide somewhere very deep inside. But a fox can always smell it.'

'We know this,' said the Queen.

'I cannot smell any life in him. I'm sorry.'

'You should be ashamed to say that,' the Queen told him. 'You shouldn't give up. He is your friend.'

'I've lost other friends,' the fox responded darkly.

Pertelot didn't know how to argue against this. 'The world is new!' was all she could think to say. 'Why is this happening, when the world is new!' She looked around rather desperately, as if she expected the Great Cat to come back and help them.

'I think the world is us,' said her husband gently.

'Oh Ragnar, Ragnar!'

During this exchange, Cy the tabby had been prowling restlessly up and down, stopping every so often to knead the bleak ground by Tag's head, while she purred in a confused way.

Now she whispered, 'Don't die, Ace. I got something so good to tell you. Don't be dead.'

The fox got up and tried to comfort her, and all four of them stood looking down at Tag for a long time. 'I remember when he was a kitten,' Loves A Dustbin said. 'He was in trouble the moment he left the house. But he never stopped loving the world.' At last, they became weeks went by. The kittens thrived. Leonora Whitstand Merril insisted, "I hear them down there at night." If we had listened to her then, and asked ourselves what to do, would things have been any different? Who can tell? What is certain is that neither of them could get the upper hand. Neither of them dared relinquish the struggle for more than a second or two. Yet both were preoccupied by their own thoughts. The Alchemist, who, in the instant of his downfall, had at last understood the meaning of what he had done, began to wonder how he might locate and destroy the Golden Cat. Majicou, while he had known all along that, for his old enemy, the moment of success would be the moment of defeat, had not expected to share it. Now, both of them realized that while the kittens remained alive, the Alchemist was not safe.

'In that moment, it all began again.

'Within the vortex, they began to use the wild roads, each in his way. They sent out proxies to do their work for them. 'The Alchemist worked through human beings and animals – Kater Murr was one of his proxies, and there will have been others in every city in the world. Majicou was less successful at this, though, as he and his opponent spun and boiled along the bottom of the sea, he was able to enlist the services of Ray the fish, who subsequently befriended Cy. Hoping in his impatience and despair to speak more directly to us, he began to send us a message: the Triangular Sign . . .

'Could they keep their thoughts and intentions from one another, those implacable enemies, as they struggled within the vortex? We can't know. Item by item, they renewed their connection with the world above. It was a connection tenuous, intermittent, hard to control. Their plans could be blown awry by a strong wind. Only one thing remained hard and certain: where one went, the other must inevitably follow. What one tried to make, the other tried to undo. That was how things stood the day the first of the kittens disappeared.'

Tag was silent for a time, ordering his thoughts.

'Even then,' he went on, 'I knew that something was wrong with the wild roads. That was how I put it, and how

'Imagine yourself in the dark – beneath the earth or under the sea. You cannot speak. You dare not stop struggling. You are locked forever in the coils of your own duality. Your enemy is you. You are your enemy. Your sole means of speech is through a fisherman; or a fish. The Majicou could only try to tell us what he had always known. None of Pertelot's kittens was the one the Alchemist sought. This wasn't some small piece of magic: to change the world for ever, *all three* would be needed. That is what the Sign meant: three sides for three kittens and the three different qualities, the three interwoven dances, which would bring down the Great Cat – that great rising sun at the apex of the pyramid. What seems so obvious to us as we stand here now, he was trying to tell us all along. The fish took you to Egypt so that you could read the old story, how Atum-Ra and Isis were beloved of the Great Cat. Majicou hoped that, of all of us, you two had the best chance of understanding. He may have tried to be there to talk to you himself: if so, he brought the whirlwind down on you instead. He was yoked to it: so how could he not?'

He was silent for a moment. Then he said, 'I shall miss the Majicou. He taught me as well as he could in the time he had left to him. He fought a long hard fight for cats, and I don't believe he foresaw – though he foresaw a great deal – how he would suffer before She released him from his task.'

Pertelot Fitzwilliam shivered.

'The Great Cat was behind it all,' she said.

Tag relied, 'The Great Cat is always behind it all.'

'It is over now, though.'

'It is.'

'Things are made anew.'

'They are.'

'You looked after us well, Mercury.'

'We looked after each other, Pertelot Fitzwilliam.'

Even as this exchange took place, the green dream was settling into the world. Sometimes it was visible, sometimes it was not. One moment, the hilltop was bare. The next it had been clothed with soil, and the soil put forth shoots like the rear, his pink tongue flapping like a yard of ribbon as he stared about in amazement at the new morning – made their way down to the ruins of the oceanarium. The fish-tank had survived against all odds, and was now laced with grape ivy and convolvulus. Down through the water struck shafts of sunshine so massy and palpable that the fishes seemed to turn like dancers between the columns of a temple. Honeysuckle and clematis wound the treads of the spiral stair. Ragnar and Pertelot trod and purred and kneaded. They felt that they had survived against the odds too. To mark this event, and give it its proper weight, they circled the fish-tank three times; and the Golden Cat twined itself between them as they went. Now it had three selves, now it had one. Isis, Odin and Leonora Whitstand Merril merged and flickered into a single tall lean unfocused shape which wound back and forth between the King and Queen like living gilded banner.

All this time, Sealink and Mousebreath had been rather shyly standing to one side, each eyeing the other but making no overtures. They were both so changed by their experiences they hardly recognized one another. He could not believe how tired she looked, or how different she smelled. She couldn't quite get to grips with the Animal X in him. It had been long hard roads for both of them, and there were many stories left to be told, and neither of them understood just yet the things that had happened. So they stood around on opposite edges of the celebration, full of awkwardness, separated by death and adventure and perhaps pride; and she was a little angry with him for not coming forward and making things easy, and he was a little angry with her for the same reason; and both of them were a little afraid.

'Won't you come and talk to him?' suggested Tag to the calico.

'Tell you the truth, honey, I can't quite believe he's there,' said Sealink, in rather too loud a voice. 'Last time I hear anything, he's dead. Now he comes back with a split personality.'

She washed her tail energetically.

'I got one or two things to tell you, too,' he admitted, thinking of Amelie.

And they fell to rubbing heads, and rolling about like kittens in the sun and the smell of the sea. After that, they walked off together for a while, talking ten to the dozen, down through the village towards the harbour. Their tails were straight up and tip-curled. Her great furry haunches rolled like a ship at sea; he gave them an appreciative look. The sidelong glances she cast him when she thought he wasn't looking would change your views on love. His mismatched eyes caught every one of them; and you could hear him say:

'It's nice ter come back from the dead. I might do it more often.'

'You'll get the chance, if you ain't true.'

The Dog had watched all these events with puzzlement. There had been some bad weather in the night. You couldn't deny that. Cats had made a lot of fuss about the weather and run about shouting at one another: you couldn't deny that, either. There is never any sense in courting trouble: the Dog had done the sensible thing and waited it all out in a doorway in the village. Even so, it had got wet. Now it waited again until Sealink and Mousebreath were safely out of sight, then set itself to limp slowly to the top of the hill. There it cast about. If its eyes were no longer good, its nose was still reliable.

'A dog can take its time about things,' it thought as it went. 'That is another thing about a dog.'

After several false casts it found Tag, and stood there panting a little in front of him, the smell of its coarse damp coat overpowering the odours of honeysuckle and convolvulus. Its body rocked backwards and forwards.

'You are the New Majicou,' it said.

'I am.'

'I do not know the names of all these other cats.'

'No.'

'They look like cats to me, whatever you want to call them. One cat looks very much like another.'

345

size of intakes on a jumbo jet (as Sealink might have put it).
Something large had arrived.

'It's Ray!' cried Cy the tabby. 'He's back!'

To the bemused Dog she confided, 'When Ray gets here,
that's when the party really begins.' She added, 'He's a fish,
but he's, like, also my friend.' And she ran up the spiral
stairs to welcome him.

Below, a curious silence prevailed. The Dog continued to
stare expectantly at Tag. The King and Queen stared
puzzledly at the Dog. Then the Dog seemed to become
aware of the fox. It studied him as closely as it could. It said,
'This is not a cat. But it is not a dog, either.'

Loves A Dustbin hung his tongue out amusedly.

'Don't get trapped in simple oppositions,' he advised, 'if
you intend to enjoy life's rewards.'

Hearing only the word 'reward', the Dog forgot him
instantly and turned its attention back to Tag. Just then, Cy
came down the stairs. In five minutes, all the joy had gone
out of her.

'What is it?' said Tag.

'Oh, I love that Ray-guy, but sometimes he's just so *irri-
tating*. I ask him to the wedding, but no, he wants to go on
somewhere else. I say, "Where's that?" He says, "Just down
the road." I say, "Oh yes?" And he says, "It's the stars,
Little Warm Sister. It's out among the stars!" I go, "What?
What's out there?" Tag, he can't even say what! So I go,
"No way, Ray, I never liked it much the first time." There's
nothing out there but cold and like that.'

She shook her head.

'These fish!' she said.

'I would have stayed here anyway,' she told Tag. 'Even
without the special reasons I got now.' Nevertheless, she
seemed bereft. 'I'll miss that Ray, when he goes swimming
back to the stars for kicks. I never had a fish for a friend
before. I just ate them.'

'He'll come back,' Tag reassured her.

'Oh yes, in another thousand years.'

Suddenly Tag had an idea.

'Ask him not to leave for a moment,' he told her.

'I don't know what people have got against my food,' said Cy angrily. 'Well, there's one more thing, *Ace* – ' here she gave Tag a significant look ' – then the cupboard's closed.' And she drew forth her *chef-d'oeuvre*: two squares of milk chocolate still in their blue foil wrapper.

'This is all we have,' said the Queen to the Dog, with the generosity of the very royal.

The Dog sniffed the chocolate.

'Mm,' it said. 'That's nice.'

With its great blunt claws and yellow teeth, it stripped off the silver paper, its muzzle creasing up, its lips wrinkling. Then it ate the chocolate. It ate very slowly and carefully, so as to prolong the sensation as long as it could, looking up at the cats every so often and chewing with its mouth open. Then, with equal care, it licked the ground where the chocolate had been, relishing every crumb. Its energetic tongue propelled the silver paper into the air, where, caught by a breeze from the sea, it seemed to turn into a small butterfly with blue wing-tips. Cy chased off after it, clapping her paws in the air. She looked like a kitten again. The Dog watched her with something like appreciation on its face.

'Well?' asked Tag. 'Was that good?'

The Dog considered.

'It was. It was good. One thing about a dog – a dog knows about chocolate. Now,' it said, 'for the stars.'

It got itself turned about in an almost lively way on its three legs, and stared up the spiral steps. Its gaze carried on past the rusty viewing platform and into the sky.

'This is a good reward,' it said to Tag. 'Anything could be out there.' It lowered its voice. 'I would never admit this to any cat but you: but it can get boring, being so dependable.'

With great effort, blunt claws clicking and scraping, it made its way up the spiral staircase to the viewing platform. There it stood panting for a moment, looking around as if it might change its mind. Then it seemed to shrug. There was a flash brighter than the sun. The oceanarium water thickened to pearl. When it cleared again, fish and dog had gone.

*